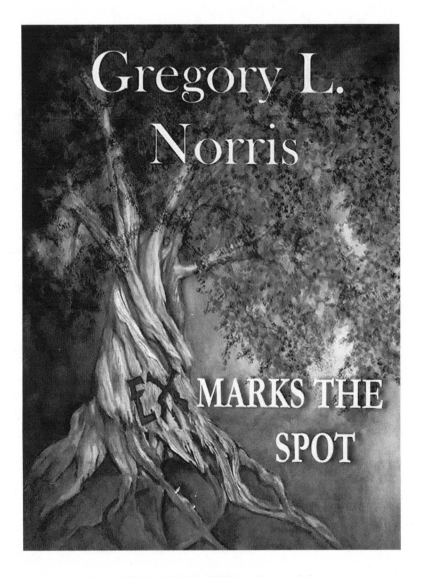

Gregory L. Norris

MARKS THE SPOT

"Mr. Norris is a master at creating a sexy, supernatural romance that takes you on an exciting journey through time. Oliver is a mess. Married to Bradley, he has never gotten over the death of Steve, his first love ten years earlier. On the anniversary of Steve's death, Oliver feels tortured, trapped between a living man who he loves and a ghost. He does go back, but discovers if you change the past, other things change too. Throughout, Mr. Norris' descriptive narrative is gorgeous, the dialogue real and as the story unfolds, you root for Oliver to make the right choices."

—**Roxanne Dent**, author of supernatural fantasies and romances, *The Grimaldi Chronicles: The Janus Demon, The White Fog, The American Heiress,* and *The Twelve Days of Christmas*

"Being very familiar with Mr. Norris' short stories, I was extremely pleased and eagerly anticipated reading his latest novel, Ex Marks the Spot. Gregory's prose is always deeply embedded in the human psyche and how it is affected by the supernatural world. And this story is no exception. A man haunted by his past love and loss finds a way to go back and possibly re-write history. Along this path, Mr. Norris takes us deeply into the meanings of love and consequences of actions taken. A thoroughly engrossing read from beginning to end, you will not be able to put it down until you've walked the path."

—**Actor/Producer Daniel Lench**, *Circle, Patient Seven, Love Exclusively,* and *Dark Web*

EX MARKS THE SPOT

Gregory L. Norris

Woodhall Press
Norwalk, CT

woodhall press

Woodhall Press, 81 Old Saugatuck Road, Norwalk, CT 06855
WoodhallPress.com

Cover design: Judi A. Calhoun
Layout artist: LJ Mucci

Library of Congress Cataloging-in-Publication Data available

ISBN 978-1-949116-51-9 (paper: alk paper)
ISBN 978-1-949116-52-6 (electronic)

First Edition

Distributed by Independent Publishers Group
(800) 888-4741

Printed in the United States of America

To Bruce

Chapter 1

As the ten-year anniversary of Steve Ranley's death neared, I fell into a deepening gloom, a kind of fugue state that left me feeling like I was walking through neck-deep water.

"You okay?" Bradley asked.

I'd been aware of him but in a disconnected way. Aware that the shower had turned off, of him moving around and getting ready for his shift at the Friday Harbor police station and the scent of soap on his skin carrying through our little house near the big woods.

"Oliver?"

I blinked. "Yeah, fine," I lied and rose from the bistro table on the screened-in porch for another cup of coffee—not sure why, since the first sat in my gut like acid.

He attempted to follow me, which I both admired and resented. I'd never been much of a public mourner. As I poured, not making eye contact, I sensed his gaze on me, seeing truths I couldn't voice.

"You sure?"

"Yup," I snapped, a bit too quickly, another tell to support my deception.

"All right," Bradley said.

Tall, his beard perfect, dressed in his crisp police uniform, he moved closer, and though I didn't want his nearness to feel like an invasion, it did. He lowered and kissed the back of my head. I closed my eyes. My next breath came with difficulty.

"Don't forget, your dad's coming over tonight for dinner, so don't be late," he said.

I cleared my throat. "He only visits to hang out with you, so no worries."

"Oliver," he admonished.

"Fine."

I downed my second cup in one pull, suffering the jolt as the acid landed in my tortured stomach.

"If you need me—"

I nodded. "I'll call. Thanks, babe."

"Love you, babe," Bradley said on his way out the door.

"Yeah, me too," I said, but he was beyond hearing me by then.

I waited for the sound of his truck's ignition and then the familiar drone as he drove away from the house. In the stillness that followed, a mourning dove cooed its melancholy song from somewhere in the surrounding trees. I recalled that mourning doves were monogamous creatures, that they mated with one and only one partner for life. One love. I was trapped between two—a living man and a ghost. Steve was like a scar over a wound that had never healed.

I switched off the coffee maker and went about the rest of the morning's minutiae, sensing a pressure that seemed determined to submerge and drown me. I tried to drink in the beauty of my surroundings, a secret ritual I performed every morning. The bungalow, which we'd named Blackberry Corners, spread around me, its walls decorated in botanical prints, its furniture a mix of new and antique with exquisite attention to detail and care. Sunlight streamed through the canopy of branches bordering our two-plus acres backed against the far southern end of the Old Coach Conservation Woods.

The air was perfumed from so many late-summer plantings in bloom, the heritage blackberries among them. In its presentation, this day ranked among the most beautiful in all of history. But everywhere I turned lurked shadows to stain that beauty. While picking up my cell and keys, the sadness inside me doubled, and tears invaded my eyes, unable to be stopped.

Ten years. For a frightening instant, time around me seemed to dissolve, and I was there again the day after it happened, staring without blinking at the fresh gouges torn into the hide of that cursed tree. And the blood—Steve Ranley's blood, which I was certain the giant oak had lapped up on the rainy night at the end of that lost August.

Wiping my eyes, I headed out of the house, intending to drive to the nursery. I followed the usual course down Harbor Road, but when the sign for Friday Harbor Garden Center rose before me, I kept on going and didn't stop until I reached the cemetery.

I set the sprigs of blackberry cuttings—thorns, leaves, and berries—at the base of the gray granite headstone, leaving a few drops of my blood in tribute as well. I drew in a deep breath. The morning's building humidity mixed into the sweetness of newly mowed lawn.

"I shouldn't be here," I said aloud to the dead man buried six feet under me. "But then again, neither should you, even though you're the past and I know Bradley's the present. But I keep getting the two times confused."

A low wind gossiped across the cemetery, stirring the fragrance of grass and sunlight. Soon the summer would end. August 30. It said so in the deep gouges etched into Steve Ranley's headstone.

Summer. Life. In a way, my life had ended with his, and I might as well have been in his ride the night of the accident, dead against that towering oak.

But I wasn't. I was still alive, at least in the physical sense. Only I wasn't complete and hadn't been for some time.

Ten years.

I bowed my head, straightened, and drove off to the nursery.

My facade fixed in place, I parked my hybrid in the usual spot, got out, and marched into the main building.

"You're late," Rudy said.

"I own the place—I can show up or not show up when-ever I want," I countered. "That's why I have you to manage things."

He flashed a snarky grin and pulled me behind the sparse cover of a flowering hibiscus. "Heads up, we're on CPL alert."

I connected dots and sighed. "The Crazy Plant Lady's back?"

"*Shhh*, she might hear you," he said.

"Don't you have orders to take care of?"

"They're being taken care of. Some of us got here two hours ago."

"*Boss*, remember?"

I playfully smacked his arm and continued through the main building, past the neat rows of houseplants and potted palms and into the greenhouse, which now contained the first of the autumn mums and the last of summer's annuals in hanging baskets. The air was rich, warm, the landscape bright. Among the golds and whites of chrysanthemums and the royal purples and blood reds of petunias, I located a shock of silver hair and the slight woman clad in a peasant dress and flats.

"Can I help you with anything?" I asked.

Ms. Cathy Burch, who used to teach Sophomore Biology at Friday Harbor High School, whirled away from a table bearing a few unsold marigolds and fixed me with a look. "You're overwatering them."

"We are? Marigolds like water."

"Not that much water."

"Who told you?" I asked—a mistake.

"*They* did, that's who."

I considered her—a broken, strange little woman who spoke to plants.

"Would you like them?" I asked.

"Them?" she parroted.

"The marigolds. Take them. All of them. Free," I sighed. "They remind me too much of the Mexican Day of the Dead anyway."

I turned and started back toward the main building. There were orders to be filled—cedar mulch and ground stone and trees to be delivered and planted, rolls of sod to lay, and, likely, the usual flow of customers to serve.

"Wait," she said.

I stopped and tipped a look over my shoulder. "What?"

Ms. Burch gathered up the marigold pots in her tiny hands and clutched them against her breast. "Last night, I had a dream; only I think it was more of a vision. About you. About trees. I'm convinced the way back and forward again is through the rings."

"The rings?"

"The rings of trees, each ring marking one year. One year's growth and energy in terms of sunlight and the cosmic spark that first gave life to the universe." She narrowed her eyes on me. "Travel through time is possible."

Then Ms. Burch, the Crazy Plant Lady, hastened away with her score of pungent flora. I stood frozen, absorbing her words, which were crazy, and I judged them as such. Still . . .

I heard Rudy arguing with her near the exit.

"It's okay," I called across the distance. "I gave them to her."

Without warning, my legs renounced their strength. I made it over to the table, emptied of marigolds, and set my hands down on the rough wooden top for support.

Rudy appeared. "How am I supposed to retire early on hypothetical big bonuses if you keep giving away the company's profits?"

"It was just a bunch of stinky old marigolds. Besides, they spoke to her."

"You okay, Boss?"

I sucked down a breath of the green air and righted. "Sure."

The answer was no truer than the lie I'd given to Bradley an hour earlier. My balance recovered, I continued to the main building.

"She used to grow weed in the high school greenhouse, along with tomato plants and a few Venus flytraps," I said. "I never tried any—the weed, that is—but I heard it was pretty robust stuff."

"That explains a lot," Rudy said.

Time travel through the rings of trees. Ms. Burch was whacked. She had been then, when she had taught biology. Everyone knew it. I remembered my own sophomore experience—nothing outstanding. I'd gone through the halls of learning with blinders on the same way I had through life. I hadn't come into my own identity until the summer I was eighteen.

The summer I spent with Steve Ranley.

On the drive home, light rained down through the trees, forming mosaics inside the car. The air was sweet from the harbor and perfumed by the vast green spaces that surrounded me.

I remembered what Bradley said before his departure from the house. My father. They would barbecue together; talk sports, work, and life. As usual, I'd be the third wheel, an afterthought. Not that I minded. That same summer with Steve and our brief, doomed love, my secret had gotten out and had created an ugly rift between Lawrence Canfield and me.

I drove slowly, in no hurry to join them. The day's austere significance threatened to engulf me, pressing down with crushing weight. Ten years earlier and about forty-eight hours from now, Steve would be having a similar argument with his father, Lloyd Ranley. Whatever had been said between them remained a mystery.

I'd called Steve right after it happened, right as he'd stormed out of their house on Dean Avenue on the other side of town—the other side of the conservation woods, which stretched for miles through the middle of Friday Harbor.

"*Can't talk*," he'd barked into the phone.

He'd hung up. And that was that.

I turned the wheel, passed into the cathedral of tall trees that rose on either side of our section of the road, and slowed at the entrance to Blackberry Corners. We'd found the little house in desperate need of TLC on a warm May afternoon four years before and had renovated it from the foundation up to its new metal roof. Most of the ornamental gardens growing around the driveway owed to unsold, end-of-summer stock that would have otherwise perished but now thrived here. As for the blackberries . . . those were an homage to a memory from that other time and place, before Bradley Steven MacIntyre.

A memory from my summer with Steve Ranley.

13

I pulled up the long driveway and parked my ride beside Bradley's truck and my father's convertible. Smoke billowed from the corner of deck where Bradley's grill dominated—steaks, according to the mouthwatering aroma. The two men stood with cold longnecks in hand huddled close to the flames. I should have been upset that my father liked my husband more than me. But I wasn't. Bradley, in his cargo shorts, T-shirt, and flip-flops, and my father—cargo shorts, T-shirt, white crew socks, and sneakers—were a snapshot of a real-life dad and son enjoying beer and barbecue.

"You're late," Bradley said as I approached.

I flashed a smile, aware of its fake fit. "So everyone keeps telling me today. Got held up at work."

"Don't you own that place?" my father asked, adding just enough of *that* tone for me to hear the insult.

"So I keep telling them."

I entered the house, did my usual giving of thanks for the pomegranate accent wall in the living room that Bradley had painted to perfection, the pair of antique bronze horses in the home office that had been my grandfather's and which I'd always vowed would be on display when I owned my own place, and the painting of blackberries and brambles above the overstuffed living room sofa.

The screen door to the porch banged into place. Bradley ambled in, beer in one hand.

"Hey," he said.

I met him and offered a kiss in greeting, one of those quick ones. My dad had gotten okay with us over the years—it didn't hurt that he considered Bradley like a son—but I still wasn't sure he could handle open displays of genuine affection.

"What do you have to go with the steaks?" I asked.

Bradley shrugged. "I dunno."

"You were just planning on steak?"

"What's wrong with that?"

I tsked, crossed to the kitchen, and pulled the antique harvest basket from the top of the fridge along with the clean scissors. The vegetable garden stretched for a quarter of an acre along the little brook that meandered out of the woods and marked our northern property line. The plot produced far more fresh food than the two of us could hope to enjoy, especially the bounty of tomatoes in August, so we donated extra produce to the local food pantry that served Friday Harbor and our three nearest neighboring towns.

I gathered plump red tomatoes, cucumbers, and various types of leaf lettuce along with arugula and fresh basil. I pulled scallions, a golden pepper off the vine, and an eggplant, which would roast well on the grill. I sliced that first, set it on a plate, and sprinkled it with olive oil, salt, and pepper.

I handed the plate to Bradley. "I'm making us a salad."

"Of course you are—you and your healthy rabbit food," my father said.

"At least you never had to force me to eat my vegetables, did you, Dad?"

We ate, talked, and laughed some. Mostly I watched the clock and the setting sun, each telling me the time to that dark anniversary was coming closer, closer. More than once, I caught myself holding my breath, unaware I was doing it until the last sip of air bottled up inside my lungs turned volcanic.

My father left, and, as was the custom, we parted ways with nods. For Bradley, saying goodbye involved handshakes and a lightness in my father's stern expression that was never there for me. I was down with it. We'd never been close and never would be.

While I was washing the dishes, Bradley came up behind me, intending to help.

"No, I've got this," I said.

"Sure?"

I was. He kissed the back of my neck, and I pretended to want it. My entire body felt full of pins and needles, that sensation when one of your limbs falls asleep from being at an awkward angle, only it was all over, even inside me. I met his kiss directly.

"You up for a date?" he whispered, using our secret couple's language for sex.

"It's late," I said.

Saying nothing more, he backed away. Less than a minute later, I heard the TV running in our bedroom. I stood, staring out the kitchen window into the growing darkness. The world turned in its orbit, and the days, hours, minutes, and seconds continued to run out.

Chapter 2

In a daze, I slipped out of bed. Bradley drowsed on his side of the mattress. The TV ran on mute—late enough that whatever program he'd fallen asleep to was long over, with an ad for restoring hair growth now running on the screen.

I made my way through the dark house, not sure why and, in retrospect, not fully in control of my faculties. It had been some time since I'd gone sleepwalking. There were instances that I remembered vividly. The last, three years ago, soon after the renovations to Blackberry Corners were completed, I went looking for what the weatherman promised was the first snow of the season. I didn't even care for snow. Winter weather was the quiet time for the nursery after Christmas. Worse, it was desolate for someone like me who loved the green of spring and summer as much as I did. But I walked—naked—out of bed sometime just after one o'clock in the morning and would have continued out of the house had I not bumped my thigh into the dining table on the way by, shocking myself out of the trance. I told Bradley I needed to take a whiz when he called to me. Quick thinking, sure.

Not so on this night, now little more than fifteen hours from the ten-year anniversary of Steve Ranley's death. I made it past the table, through the back door to the sunporch, somehow managing to disable the house alarm in my zombified state. Then outside, across the driveway, over rough pine tree roots and the edge of the wood line. The pain inflicted by stepping on stones and sharp twigs should have woken me but didn't. I continued through the garden, the blackberry patch, and to the brook.

Every summer, the brook dried up, only to surge back in October when the autumn rain resurrected it from the dead. It was gone now, a brown depression winding through the woods. The brook marked our northern property line, but we were located at the southern boundary of the conservation woods. Hemlocks and dozens of other species of tree roots purified the water that flowed through those hundreds of acres.

I moved to the very edge, my bare toes just touching the bas-relief proof that a brook even existed there. A low, warm wind stirred through the trees, smelling of shadowy, green realms and mystery.

"*Oliver*," a voice whispered, male, though I wouldn't exactly label it as human.

I turned in its direction, eyes wide, my pulse in a sudden panic. "Who—?"

I sensed I was being watched from the darkness, the trees. No answer came, not in words, at least. A long moment after my question, a sound reached from the brooding woods—a building trickle of water, according to my ear. More and more, the water poured out and flowed toward me. The rush surged closer. The brook had returned early.

A minor tidal wave swept out of the forest, filling the brook's depression. Water sluiced past, soaking my feet. Only the deluge registered as hot and thick, and when I looked down, I saw that what I had mistaken for water was blood.

"*If you interfere . . .*" the voice threatened.

I gasped myself awake in my bed, soaked in sweat and barely able to trap the scream behind my teeth. To my horror, the cadence of water trickling and tumbling continued—no mere echo of the nightmare, I soon realized. Rain spilled off the metal roof. Nauseous, I sat up, the sound of the storm ferocious.

"Babe?" Bradley asked in a sleepy voice.

"Go back to bed," I said. "It's raining—I'm gonna close windows."

Eyes shut, he smiled, nodded, and rolled over. The TV, I saw, ran muted. Some ridiculous ad for male hair restoration showed "Before" and "After" photos. Outside the house, thunder rumbled.

Rain pounded down from the sky, the kind of cascade that makes it impossible to see things even when they're directly in front of you.

It had rained that day too, ten years ago. The day hadn't started out overcast, no—the morning of August 30 had dawned sunny, hot, and bright. I might have been the only person on the planet who remembered such useless but also vital trivia. For most of the afternoon, there wasn't a single cloud in the sky. I know this for a fact, as I know most of the details of that summer down to atoms and molecules. To me, they are unforgettable. Because of Steve and what we shared.

The storm had swept in out of nowhere, one of those violent summer soakers that springs forth without much warning, sends the TV networks into such a frenzy that they cut into regular programming to warn of dangerous wind, hail, and possible power outages. The eerie coincidence that the dark anniversary should fall on a day with driving rain left me shivery despite the morning's heat. The body doesn't forget, and mine hadn't.

"No coffee today?" Bradley asked.

"No."

He hovered, leaning a hip against the sink, and I sensed his nervousness. For days he'd tiptoed around the subject of the anniversary of Steve Ranley's death. I had to commend him for understanding my misery.

"Want to talk about it?" he asked.

I shook my head, picked up my keys and cell, and started for the door. For once, I'd be early. That would both please and shock Rudy.

"*Oliver*," he called.

I halted.

"I know what this day is, what it means," he said behind me.

I didn't turn, didn't answer.

"Don't you think it'll help if we talk about it? About him and what happened—how it's eating you alive?"

But I couldn't. Unable to answer, I continued out the door, into the rain. Then I was driving, wondering if I was taking Harbor Road in the right direction. Or if I was even still *on* the road.

At one point, the intensity subsided enough for me to reach the garden center.

"You'll pay for the night's sins in the morning," I grumbled, aware of the warmth in the greenhouse but feeling cold all over.

"What's that?" Rudy asked from across the room.

I waved it off. "Nothing."

The words had slipped out of me before I could stop them. I'd said them in that other, lost summer ten years behind me. The chill hanging onto my flesh deepened.

"I'll be back in a minute," I said, suddenly unable to breathe.

I hurried out of the greenhouse and cut through the side door connecting to the main outdoor nursery space. That area was a magical forest of trees, shrubs, and neat rows of flowers in pots interspersed with bird fountains, marble and granite garden benches, and statuary. The sweet fragrance of rain on flowers greeted my senses. I could breathe again.

I hadn't been standing there long when a flutter of movement teased the corner of my eye. I turned toward my left in time to see it vanish into the thin mist left over from the rain. I pursued, tromping down the path between potted Japanese maples and ornamental cherry trees, the last of the season's blue and pink hydrangeas, and hollyhocks, obscenely huge and covered in blood-red blossoms.

I came to the end of the aisle. No one was there except for a garden statue of a man, handsome in depiction, posed like a classic athlete from Ancient Greece. His skin was the gray of a ghost.

I met Bradley Steven MacIntyre two years after Steve Ranley died. I was working full-time at the garden center and had positioned myself to take over as manager and, a year later, to buy the place from Jim Fenster when he retired. Bradley was my age and working a summer job as a lifeguard at the harbor, not really sure what he wanted to do after the season ended. I suggested the police academy one morning, when we paid for the previous night's sins. We dated, moved in together, and married. We bought an old, tired fixer-upper on the south side of the conservation woods and fixed it up.

I loved him, yes. But the truth was, our relationship had never been only about the two of us. It had always been a threesome—Bradley, me, and a dead man.

After the incident near the statue, I called out early and returned home. Mist hung over Blackberry Corners. From the woods, a bird cried out. I'd returned to a haunted no-man's-land.

Suffering guilt, I entered the house and headed directly to the small second bedroom at the back, where bookshelves lined walls and an antique desk that Bradley had restored formed our library and office. I pulled a hardcover volume from the bottom shelf of the case that displayed my books. It was my senior yearbook.

I carried it over to the desk and laid it out on top of the polished tiger maple. I flipped through the succession of meaningless captures of cheerleaders and football players, only to flip back. There, in black and white, was the Crazy Plant Lady holding a pot with a Venus flytrap in one hand, aiming the pointer of her other toward its spiny open mouth. Utter cheeseball; I shook my head and then resumed flipping.

There I was, eighteen years old, my hair in a mop. It was customary to list beneath each student's senior photo their immediate plans—what college they'd been accepted to or if they were joining the workforce. Mine read: "Going to figure out the meaning of life."

It read like pure snark, only I wasn't the class clown, and the statement was valid. Back then I didn't know and, oh, how I wanted the answer, *needed* it.

Past "Canfield," I flipped ahead to "Ranley." As I neared my destination, a barely-remembered host of relics spilled out of confinement. One was a little card and its matching green envelope, the other an intact photograph from a camera I still had on a shelf in the closet of this very room, only they no longer made the film for it.

The card showed rich clusters of purple blackberries and green leaves reproduced from a watercolor painting. I remembered that I'd planned to give it to Steve along with a message declaring my love for him. But that hadn't happened. The card was still blank.

The photograph was grainy, poorly lit despite the flash, and clearly from a bygone era, the decade identified by the quality and color of the film. In it, Steve and I were posed for an early version of a selfie, the camera in his hands.

"*Here, let me,*" he said in my thoughts. Cool. A man always confident, always in control—except at the end, when the universe wrestled that away from him.

I gazed down at his graduation picture. He faced the camera with a tough guy's expression—no smile, almost no emotion apart from that in his eyes. His dark hair was neat, in an athlete's cut. The pinstriped button-down shirt, tie, and suit jacket fit him as though his clothes loved his body. He was so handsome that it physically hurt to look at him for too long, like staring directly at the sun. After a few seconds, I'd go blind.

But I had no real worries on that count. My eyes resumed watering. The world around me submerged in a fresh deluge, this one inside the walls of the house.

"Oh, Steve," I sobbed. And then I howled it to the limit of my lungs.

Sound stirred behind me. I spun in the seat toward the door, convinced that the specter chasing me was back. Worse, in my grief I hadn't heard Bradley enter the house. He stood at the threshold of the office dressed in his police uniform. Through the watery veil over my eyes, I could see his hurt.

"Rudy called me. He was worried about you," Bradley said.

I sniffled, tried to speak, at first unsuccessfully. "Remind me to have a word with Rudy about keeping our professional and personal lives separate," I managed.

Bradley hovered there. "You want to tell me about it?"

"No," I said.

"Maybe I want you to. For days you've been distant and moody, and I get it. I do. I get why, Oliver. So why won't you let me help you?"

I huffed out a humorless laugh. "You can't help me. No one can, not even me!"

I stood. The yearbook spilled off the desk, dumping its exhumed relics on the *Starry Night* carpet that transformed the floor into a view of indigo sky filled with pinwheel stars. I moved to retrieve them. Bradley joined me.

I smelled his clean sweat and that note of something that reminded me of summer rain but was really his testosterone working up through skin mixed with the dregs of deodorant clinging to his uniform. Part of me, a big part, wanted to hug him and be hugged in return. To take him up on his offer and see if we could exorcize the phantom haunting our lives together, united as a couple.

But the book had landed open on the floor, and Steve Ranley's face stared up at me in black and white. The emptiness inside me doubled, making sane decisions impossible.

Steve Ranley. He was going to the police academy to be a cop. Ten years ago, not long from now according to the clock, he'd instead gone into a box and from there into the ground.

I released the yearbook and stood.

"Oliver," Bradley attempted.

"I can't," I said, rounding his body on my way out of the room.

"I know," he said. "I know you only stayed with me because of this uniform and that you were only interested in me because my middle name's Steven. But I'm not him, no matter how hard you've tried to make me into Steve Ranley."

Sometimes, all you need to do to get even with the one you love is to tell them the truth.

Saying nothing, I continued to my car and drove off, sensing that I'd never return to that house or to Bradley.

I drove, not sure of where I was going, the sides of the road blurry, cloaked in fog. A light rain fell, and the windshield wipers threatened to hypnotize me. The sane voice in the back of my mind told me to turn around, return to Blackberry Corners—more, to Bradley. We had a great life together. We had everything a couple could want. Only we weren't a couple and never had been. We were a trio.

That insane voice, the one that had been in control for days obsessing over the dark anniversary, made me ignore its counterpart. I drove around the harbor, through the quaint center of town with its cafes and few neon franchises, picked up North Main Street, and found myself in the Old Coach neighborhood where I'd grown up in my father's house.

He still lived there. I rarely went back to that place, partly because of memories associated with living there, mostly because Juniper Road connected with Dean Avenue right before it merged with South Main Street, the way back to our side of town.

The way through the conservation woods, past the cursed tree that stole Steve Ranley's life.

I turned onto Juniper Road. Number 19 rose at my left, a white ranch with black shutters. One light shone above the kitchen sink. The garage door was down, my father's precious baby tucked in for the night and cared for better than his son ever was. The lawn looked neat, and ornamental plantings I'd put in before I moved out prospered. It was the facade of a well-kept home, showing no sign of the unhappiness that had once festered within its walls.

Two houses later, Juniper Road ran out. I turned left onto Dean Avenue. As I did, the storm resumed its fury. Rain drummed across the windshield. I upped the tempo of the wipers. Night in late August arrived early, ushered in by the downpour. I traveled forward, the only car on the road—seemingly the only soul out on this most somber of anniversaries.

At my right, a succession of cookie-cutter ranch houses swept by. Two had been painted different colors since my last time here. Eventually the white split-level appeared, the last house on the road. It was pressed right up to the very edge of the conservation woods. Somewhere beyond the boundary of the house's backyard, in the tangle beyond the wood line, wild blackberries grew. Or they had a decade earlier.

The Ranleys were long gone from that house. They'd sold it after Steve's death. It was still white and looked like a giant skull in the rain.

I slowed. The car idled. The emptiness inside me widened to a chasm. Steve had died. So had I on that August day, only my body didn't know it. Ten years after the fact, death had finally caught up with me. I hadn't really been alive. Maybe I was the ghost I'd caught glimpses of in the two days leading to this night.

I shuddered. My cell phone bleated a riff from the song "I Belong to You" by Muse—my ringtone for Bradley. As the shiver finished its tumble down my backbone, I answered.

"Hi," I said.

"Hey. Where are you?" Bradley asked.

I laughed. "I'm not really sure." It was the truth.

"Come on home, Oliver. Let me help."

Warmth filled my insides, closing that giant emptiness. I smiled. "Yeah, I'd like that, babe. Okay, I'm on my way."

"I'll be here," he said.

I killed the call, steeled myself, and drove forward, past that house and its haunting memories, into the dark tunnel of the conservation woods. A quick glance at the dashboard clock showed it was 7:16. My worry surged back, and in the time it took to blink, the clock changed.

7:17.

I had crossed into the exact hour and minute when, ten years before, Steve Ranley died.

EX MARKS THE SPOT

Chapter 3

That section of road bending south dipped significantly before leveling out again maybe a tenth of a mile farther up. I wasn't traveling fast on my own, but the outside world sped past as I hydroplaned down the incline. The gods had re-created the exact conditions to both the letter and time of Steve Ranley's accident.

I tapped the brakes. Instead of slowing, the hybrid canted center left. I compensated with the wheel. My tires left the pavement and banged over uneven ground. Tree branches clawed at the side of the car.

Right before I plowed into the tree—that same cursed oak—I saw it rising up from the earth, a giant. In that glimpse of less than a second, it towered over me, a monster with numerous gnarled arms, all of which waited to reach down and tear me apart like the trees in a nightmare. Not that it needed to. I shot a look back down in time to see the front of the car aimed at its colossal trunk, which had already feasted once on human blood and would again.

Deafening thunder erupted around and inside me as the car crumpled on impact. And then my hearing shorted out, replaced by a distant whine.

The ocean.

That's what it sounded like in the confusion that followed. The crash of waves, pounding the shoreline again and again. As my consciousness drifted in a disconnected state, my inner voice reasoned that I was hearing a million years' worth of tidal forces, all in a matter of seconds.

Dead. I had to be. Or worse, reduced to some vegetable hooked to life support. The crash of waves was really the respirator pumping oxygen into my lungs. I floated in darkness, unable to identify my surroundings. Maybe this was Limbo, land of lost souls. Or an afterlife as yet unimagined. Perhaps a *before*-life.

Nothing hurt, because I felt nothing.

The pounding of tides waned. In its place was something quieter. A breeze. I felt it whisper over my skin. Willing all of my energy into this one action, I focused on the source. Like a theater curtain rising, my eyes opened. The performance they were to witness was a panorama of spilled blood. Crimson filled my vision.

The car crash, I thought. I was pinned behind the broken steering wheel, blood pouring into my eyes, surely—

Only I wasn't in pain, and the cascade of blood rippled like fabric. Because it was. I was staring across a distance of two feet at a window draped in scarlet curtains.

My mind raced. I knew those curtains, their hems a mess of frayed edges, the sewing basic, shoddy. I'd made them from fabric found at a local department store's clearance bin to replace the tired, checked Cape Cods that had hung on that window for years and always reminded me of a woman's old-fashioned bloomers.

The window was located in my old bedroom in my father's humorless house on Juniper Road.

The last thing I remembered was losing control of my car on the wet road and slamming into that monstrous oak tree. Had someone found me, pulled me from the vehicle, and taken me here to recover? That was absurd. Given the ferocity of the accident, I should have been in a hospital. Or a casket.

I flexed both arms. They were there and functioned. I did the same to my legs. Nothing ached except my belly, and that was because I was hungry. I glanced down and didn't recognize the pair of tight, white briefs that covered my crotch, the only stitch on me. I wore boxer briefs, black ones, sometimes gray. I hadn't owned white cotton briefs since—

While assessing myself, I made another observation. My arms and legs looked pale, the usual summer tan I sported from working outside was gone. Also missing was the definition of muscles. I'd bulked up as the owner of Friday Harbor Garden Center helping to load bags of mulch and trees with root balls wrapped in burlap. What I gazed down at looked like spaghetti.

I jolted upright. At first I didn't recognize the bedclothes or the bed beneath me. A captain's bed, the kind with shelves and two drawers underneath, single, the comforter and sheets beige. I hadn't slept in this bed since I was eighteen. The illusion of a breeze came from the portable fan on the nightstand, running on its highest setting. The fan, too, was a stranger until I remembered it from an earlier decade. The one from my teens.

I finished sitting up. The room performed a spin, phased out of focus, and then stabilized. I set my soles on the scuffed hardwood floor. Sensations rippled up into my flesh. It was real. All of it.

Leaning forward, I nudged aside the scarlet curtains. Beyond, the once-familiar view of my father's backyard appeared. There was the pine tree he kept threatening to take down before one storm or another did. The square, orderly patch of vegetable garden I oversaw throughout my teen years occupied the center of the property. Things were still tender and in rows, leading me to assign it a month.

"*June*," I said aloud.

Even my voice was different, younger.

I stood and shuffled to the mirrored dresser that matched the captain's bed. I wore my hair in a neat, no-nonsense buzz. The face that stared back was mine, though not the one from the present. My hair was an unruly mop, something I'd done away with in the years of my twenties and how I'd worn it in my graduation photo.

"Impossible," I sighed.

The air was thick and warm, my head full of concrete. I made it back to the bed and sat, worried I might pass out from shock.

Bradley. I was on my way home to my husband, our home at Blackberry Corners, and had crashed into that hated oak. As I forced my breaths to slow, I wondered if I'd just emerged from a dream. If I had, it was the most detailed in history. Had I imagined my life with Bradley, the house, and the nursery? No, this was the dream—it had to be!

I searched the room for my phone. It wasn't there. I opened drawers and rifled through the clothes. All of them were old, long gone—a fawn button-down I used to wear in school and the dark indigo sweater that completed the ensemble. Over to the desk in the other corner of the room. I stopped. Two things were familiar—my late grandfather's pair of bronze horses, proudly displayed on one corner of the desk, and my high school yearbook.

Hands shaking, I flipped through the pages to one I knew well. On this strange morning, the book wasn't as dog-eared as I remembered it at Blackberry Corners. There was a newness to the yearbook—I could smell the ink. At the back was Steve Ranley's graduation photo. No secret relics marked the page.

I pulled on shorts, a pale blue T-shirt, and socks. Aware of the gallop of my heart, I reached for the doorknob, not knowing what to expect. Outside my own little pocket universe could await any number of rings of Hell. Or there could be nothing but swirling vortex and the void of outer space beyond my old bedroom's hollow core door.

In a way, something worse lurked out there—the old beige shag carpet of the house's hallway.

Cautiously, I crept over it and called out, "Hello?"

No one answered.

The house brooded in silence apart from the steady hum of the fridge and the sound of a car passing down Juniper Road, audible through the open windows. I drank in my surroundings, doing a dubious version of my daily routine at Blackberry Corners. The living room was as I remembered it, with outdated sofa and matching chair, the fabric scratchy, a coffee table, and a landscape painting over the fireplace mantle, a snapshot of a room that was never visited. The same dining room table sat to the left of the kitchen. The upstairs bathroom, my father's bedroom, and the spare room completed the layout.

"Dad?" I asked the house.

Again, no response came.

I looked at the microwave clock. It was just shy of ten in the morning. According to that telling bit of information, my father would be at work. Though he always threatened to take an early retirement, he managed the marina, which meant early days.

But no, this couldn't be!

"Wake up," I said and wished the fantasy to end.

It didn't. When that failed, I pinched my own arm, twisting a big handful of skin. I winced. I was already awake.

I hastened over to the fridge. Held by a little magnet advertising our old electrician and one for a pizza place in town that had shuttered its doors before I stormed out of Blackberry Corners on August 30 in what had been my present was the printout of my father's weekly work schedule, which he'd posted from the time my mother left and it was only the two of us. He'd also taken to crossing off the days already worked, as though a kind of countdown to retirement. The weekend, anyway.

According to the last date crossed off in blue pen, it was June 27, ten years earlier.

Somehow, I'd returned to the summer I fell in love with Steve Ranley. The same summer when, at the end, he died.

I paced the house, reacquainting myself with images and scents that were strange but had one time been ordinary—the smell of the soap in the bathroom, the texture of the heavy drapes hanging in the kitchen windows. The landline phone bolted to the thin strip of wall beside the fridge. . . . I lifted it, and a dial tone poured out. If it was, indeed, the summer from ten years in my past, my grandmother was still alive. The few friends I'd known in high school were still friends before college and other circumstances sent them away.

I hadn't thought about Warren Rudd in a long while. He was the closest of those friends until I confessed to him that I was gay and the friendship fizzled out, which I was mostly okay with. Though he owned a small house in Friday Harbor, last I knew, Warren was giving the nursery a wide berth. The death of that friendship was a reflection on him and not me.

More than anything else, this meant that Steve was alive!

That realization robbed all the breath from my lungs. I spun. The house blurred. Alive? I recalled the Crazy Plant Lady's words about time travel and the rings of trees. I'd whacked into that murderous oak pretty hard. Hard enough to—

"*Die*," I said to the empty house.

Only I wasn't dead. I sat down in the nearest chair, the scratchy old dinosaur in the living room, my body rediscovering its discomfort.

Bradley—we weren't fated to meet for a few years after this point in time. I didn't even know how to contact him apart from remembering his parents once owned a hardware store in New Jersey and they traveled in the summer. After their son's graduation, they'd thought about moving to Florida, where it was warm in the winter. But now?

The one fact I knew for sure was where to find Steve Ranley. I located my sneakers, an old pair that pinched my feet. I was still in that phase of my life when I hadn't fully formed and my wardrobe reflected the awkward fit. They'd have to do.

I opened the front door. Sunlight and warmth engulfed me. The air was sweet with a blend of mowed lawn and roses from the bushes I'd planted three years before. I continued down the front steps, along the walkway, and over the driveway. From there I crossed the side of the house. Irises and narcissuses were in bloom along the garage's outer wall. In the backyard I moved past the garden and to the Discanos' stockade fence, which marked the property line.

At its corner, I cast a look through the other backyard, at the break in trees and houses that showed all the way to the end of Dean Avenue. The Ranley's split-level ranch sat in the shadows of the nearby trees. I could see their driveway from my position—two cars, one black pickup truck with a gold racing stripe detail.

That truck was Steve's—the one he'd crashed into the blood-thirsty oak.

My pulse quickened. He was still there, still alive!

I started walking, cutting across the neighbor's backyard, faster and faster. Between blinks, a phantom moved from the Ranley's front door down to the truck and got in. I hurried, running. The black truck chugged to life before I made it into view. It backed out of the driveway onto Dean Avenue then accelerated down South Main Street and was soon gone from sight.

Eyes wide, I huddled on my old bed in a fetal curl. Steve . . .

The phone rang in the kitchen, but it sounded a thousand miles away as I pondered my situation. I was counterclockwise in time, in my younger self's body, yet with my future self's mind and memory. Incredible, and yet it was.

At some untimed point in the late afternoon, the house trembled. I heard the garage door rise, and then the vibrations intensified. I accessed long-buried memories. My father was home from the marina.

I swallowed down my heart, which had jumped out of my chest and onto the back of my tongue, and got up. I joined him near the dining table, where he was going through the day's mail.

"Hey, Dad," I said.

He cut me through with a glance from the corner of his eye, answering only with a grunt.

"How was your day?" I offered.

"Long. How was yours—easy?"

I studied him, his hair only starting to go gray, his face meaner, harder to look at because it was under this roof. "Easy?" I laughed. "Um, no. Why would you think that?"

"You've been done with school for how many weeks? And you're still here every day. When are you planning to get a job? And what about after the summer? If you're not going to college—"

"Don't worry. I'm getting a job. A good one."

He narrowed his eyes. "Yeah? When?"

"A very good job. Great, in fact. At Friday Harbor Garden Center. I'm putting all my useless knowledge about plants to work."

He eyed me for another few seconds before heading to the fridge for a beer, nothing further said on the subject. I'd forgotten how cold he could be when I lived in this house.

"Dad?" I asked. "Have you seen my phone? I can't find it."

He chuckled, the sound as cold and condescending as his words. "It's on the wall."

He was right. I hadn't gotten my first phone, one of those basic pay-as-you-go jobs, until later this same summer.

My father made himself dinner and retreated behind the door to his bedroom, where the sound of the TV replaced our brief conversation. I rummaged through the fridge, fixed a Frankenstein meal of leftover parts and fresh lettuce salad from the garden, and dined alone at the table, still overwhelmed by my predicament. My life was ten years away and falling farther by the second to a distance that felt wider than an entire galaxy.

I ate the salad, picked at the remains of something and pasta, and ignored my glass of sugary soda, the only nonalcoholic beverage in the refrigerator. I got up, dumped my glass, and filled it with cold water from the tap. And as I gazed out at the afternoon, through the vista between the curtains above the sink, he appeared.

I blinked. The specter didn't vanish. My lower jaw dropped and I forgot how to breathe.

It was Steve Ranley. Out for a late afternoon walk, he turned from Dean Avenue onto Juniper Road. Basic white T-shirt. Faded blue jeans. Big, bare feet. Heavenly distraction.

The glass slipped from my hand and shattered in the sink, the thunderclap breaking my paralysis. I remembered the cannonade of my car slamming into the murderous oak and, for a fractured instant in time, was there again, behind the wheel.

The vision shorted out. I sucked in a deep, cleansing breath and my surroundings solidified. I hastened to the door and out of the house to be with him, the first great love of my life.

Chapter 4

Sunlight spilled down in splinters through breaks in the trees. The air was hotter, dryer, more bewitching. The melody of wind chimes drifted over from a neighbor's house. Some unaffected sliver of my future mind activated, telling me how crazy I was behaving as I hurried across the walkway to the driveway, my feet awkward in ill-fitting kicks.

It hadn't happened this way, not the first time. The incident that led to our brief, passionate romance had come in early July when Steve picked me up at the side of Old Coach Road when I was walking home from work—the grocery store in town, not the garden center.

I ordered myself to chill, adjusted course, and made my way to the mailbox under the guise of collecting the day's delivery.

Steve approached, moving no quicker or slower than he had when I'd spotted him from the kitchen window. It was as though I wasn't there; that I was the specter, not he. His eyes were aimed at the road, but they saw something else. As my heart hammered in my chest, he came out of his trance and noticed me.

My insides caught fire as ice formed over my skin. Steve offered me a tip of his chin, that universal greeting between males that makes instant buddies out of strangers on hoops courts and summer baseball diamonds.

I'd forgotten how handsome he was close up—handsome in a way photographs had captured but didn't really do justice. Neat, dark hair, his eyes a deep shade of blue. *Sapphires*—I'd always mused that Steve Ranley had precious gemstones for eyes. Fresh sweat glistened on his neck and arms. I caught his scent as he neared: clean skin, a note of pine, and men's deodorant. I stole a look down at his feet. They were handsome too, *sexy* in a way that part of a man's anatomy isn't normally considered. Steve Ranley was a jock, a baseball player in high school, one of the popular kids who'd never made me feel unpopular. He planned to become a cop. In the dying sunlight, he was, to me, a demigod, one step above the rest of us.

"'Sup," I said and then felt stupid.

He neared, slowed. "Not much. Just, you know . . ."

I pretended to understand what he meant. *Just displaced in time by mysterious and powerful forces? Just returned from the afterlife, from Heaven?*

". . . bored," he said.

I closed the empty mailbox and secretly drew in another breath peppered with his scent. The urge to reach out and embrace him, to tell him how happy I was to see him, how much I *loved* him, possessed me. But I fought it and succeeded.

Not so easily diminished was my growing arousal and desire for him. The heat and his nearness conspired to remind me that here, now, I was eighteen and all hormones.

"Any plans?" I asked.

"None," Steve said. He was eighteen, too, and not as sophisticated as I recalled. Not that it mattered.

"Want to hang out?" I boldly offered.

Steve's twin sapphire gaze studied me. My hopes rose, for I could see the flicker of something in his eyes. He opened his mouth. At first, no answer came. Then he blinked, flashed a nervous smile, and clapped a hand on my shoulder.

"Maybe another time, Oliver. Thanks," he said before continuing his way up Juniper Road.

I watched him go, the view from the back as spectacular as that from the front. Oh, the urge to follow him, to tell him all that I knew. But it hadn't happened like that. No, this was all different.

My flesh tingled from where he'd touched me. The scintillation spread in concentric waves, leaving me shivering all over.

I ignored the TV in my room and instead settled on the bed, my eyes aimed at the opened scarlet curtains. The night landscape glowed silver thanks to the bloated full moon hanging above the treetops.

My few minutes at the mailbox with Steve played out and replayed in my thoughts. I'd returned ten years, two full months, and a handful of days to a point in time before his death. I didn't remember that conversation at the mailbox—and surely I'd have recalled the memory of Steve in blue jeans and bare feet acting lost and in need of a friend. More than a friend, if the want in his eyes was to be trusted, as I knew from our first night together in the original timeline.

But it didn't happen this way, my inner voice repeated. *Not the first time. He picked you up on your way home from work—that crappy summer job you took to shut the old man's yap. On the road, you and Steve talked. He asked you about being gay. You denied it—until he set his hand on your knee. You never denied yourself again after that.*

That was how it happened.

At least in that other time.

Maybe it still would in this one.

The heaviness in Steve's eyes—he was questioning his sexuality. At the end of the school year and the start of summer, he was dating Lori O'Connor, one of the cheerleaders from Friday Harbor High. At this point in known history, they were still together but wouldn't be after July 4—a family party at his parents' place, after which Steve broke up with her. Our encounter was the night after that—eight days from now.

Night insects sang, their music hypnotic. A gentle breeze whispered through the window and stirred the curtains. Time wasn't as rigid as I thought, if that small but significant encounter at the mailbox was to be believed. It was fluid, and its course could be altered. Staring up at the moon, I decided that I would do all that I could to change history as I knew it.

God help me, I would save Steve. I'd stop him from driving on that night little more than two months into my new future.

I assessed my wardrobe. It was limited and embarrassing. I managed a decent enough look of cargo shorts and polo shirt and was out of my room by the time my father was ready to leave for the marina.

"Can you drop me off at the garden center on your way in to work?" I asked.

He flashed me that look, the one that said I was annoying him. My father was often annoyed first thing in the morning. Last thing at night too. But his scowl evaporated and he nodded. "That job you talked about? Think you'll get it?"

"Oh, I know I will," I said. Then, beneath my breath, I added, "*Eventually.*"

We drove down Dean, and my focus returned to the Ranley house. Steve's truck was parked in the driveway. My father drove past, clueless to the surge of emotion from the nearby front passenger's seat.

Steve's truck was there and then gone from sight. My gaze fell into the endless green beyond, the deep, shadowy realm of the conservation woods. A lightness tickled my belly as we turned down the incline. I forced my focus up, and there it was, displayed in the morning's light.

Quercus rubra—northern red oak. Only I knew it was more. The giant had feasted on human blood and was still thirsty. As we motored by, I realized this version of the murderer had yet to feed, at least regarding Steve Ranley or me. But a chill teased the short hairs at the nape of my neck as we continued, and I swore I could feel it or something diabolical hidden among its branches staring back at me.

My dad pulled into the parking lot. I looked around, disappointed at how dilapidated the place looked. I'd forgotten the old sign with its dingy paint; the overgrown strip of front lawn that would, under my ownership, be transformed to flower beds; the unpaved, rutted drive.

"Good luck," my father said.

"Thanks." I got out.

"I'm low on gas. How you planning to get home?" he asked.

Home? Home was Blackberry Corners and presently beyond my abilities to reach. He meant Juniper Road. I rolled with it. "Legs, man."

I closed the door. He drove away. Legs, for sure. I was at least another year from buying my first car. Any job I took would require walking, whether here or at Victory Supermarket. But the walking in that other reality was what transformed my legs from spaghetti to actual muscle.

I approached the entrance. On any other morning, I was the king of these five acres, but today had reduced me to a peasant. The garden center and nursery had provided an excellent life in that other timeline. The sliver of me that believed in such spiritual matters silently prayed it could do the same in this version.

I walked in through the main doors—doors I'd replaced in the years that followed. The layout was so different, with cash registers in their old, wrong places and the aisles of merchandise laid out in chaos. But the strangely pleasant funk of cedar chips, potting soil, and green things hung over the place. It smelled like the same world of my Friday Harbor Garden Center.

A girl in a red apron manned one cash register and barely acknowledged my arrival. I marched up to her and dialed back the boss in me who wouldn't have approved of that kind of behavior from one of his workers.

"Good morning," I said.

"Can I help you find something?" she asked, though it was clear she didn't care.

"Yes, an application, please."

"Application? For . . . ?"

"A job."

This brought us eye to eye. She flashed a haughty smile. "We're not hiring."

I laughed. "You're always hiring from April until the Christmas trees arrive in December."

She narrowed her eyes, and I sort of remembered her—niece or some other relative of Old Man Fenster, whom I'd worked for and gone on to buy the place from,

"Is your uncle here?" I asked.

"He's busy. We're all busy, and we're not hiring, so have a good day."

She turned away, the conversation ended. After a few seconds, I retreated through those old doors into the day's light and growing heat. Things hadn't gone like this the first time either. I'd come here in late autumn after Steve's death to unload Christmas trees and strap them to car roofs for customers. It was backbreaking work, but Jim Fenster had appreciated my efforts and kept me on through the winter.

In the known timeline, I was supposed to be bagging groceries at Victory, a miserable way to earn a paycheck. The notion bothered me more now than it ever did then because I'd grown set in my ways. The garden center was the only place I intended to work at until, like Jim Fenster, I sold it to someone younger to operate.

I started away, taking the first steps for my long walk back to Juniper Road. I still couldn't think of that house as *home*. Home was Blackberry Corners, miles and years in the opposite direction. Home was—

Bradley, I thought.

Guilt froze me where I stood. For a startling moment, the ghost that haunted me wasn't Steve Ranley but Bradley Steven MacIntyre. All the moisture evaporated from my mouth. Something had brought me back in time for a specific purpose. I could only focus on that, on saving Steve's life. I thawed and turned around, back in the direction of the garden center.

I rounded the main building, approached the area where gigantic piles of wood chips, topsoil, and crushed gravel were housed behind fences to be loaded into trucks for transport to customers. The gate was open. I continued in, passing messy rows of potted trees farther along and lawn equipment like mowers lined up beneath a wooden awning long gone from the future version of the place.

I tracked voices to a corner of the lot where pallets of grass seed and lawn fertilizer were stacked. A couple stood among the selections.

"Do you work here?" the man asked.

I shrugged.

"My lawn looks like shit," he said.

"*Hugh*," the woman admonished.

"Well, it is more brown than green," he said.

I moved to the selections, all of which had changed packaging by the summer ten years later. "You want this one. N-P-K—Nitrogen, Potassium, Phosphorous. For green grass and healthy lawns, you want a higher nitrogen content. That should de-shitify your lawn."

The man clapped my shoulder. "Thanks, man—you know your stuff."

I smiled and continued past to find myself under the watchful scrutiny of Jim Fenster, a tall man with a beer gut who was mean but mostly fair, and closing in on the end of his time running the garden center. He didn't know that yet.

"Impressive," he said, arms folded in a defensive posture, his body language impossible to misread. "But would you care to tell me who you are?"

I extended my hand. "Oliver Canfield, Mister Fenster. I'm here for a job."

He laughed. "I don't need any extra help at the moment, even if you do seem to know a thing or two about the lawn and garden business."

After it became clear he wasn't planning to take my offered hand, I withdrew it.

"Let me tell you why you should reconsider," I said. "I know a lot about plants, gardens, lawns, and landscaping."

"Oh?" he said, unimpressed.

I accessed the wealth of useless information imprinted on my gray matter. "Orchids. You can't over- or under-water them. To be safe, you press your pointer finger an inch into the potting soil to see how damp it is. But orchids really need humidity to thrive, so you take them into the bathroom when you shower. That's the difference between healthy orchids and dead ones."

"*Orchids,*" Fenster said. "You're not really making a big case for yourself. What I need is someone who can haul bags of lawn fertilizer out to car trunks."

"Fine," I said.

"You don't look like you can handle ten pounds of cat litter."

I shot him a look, returned to the couple near the pallet, and pulled the top bag from the stack. "Let me get this for you."

Fenster was partly correct. That fifty-pound bag of fertilizer felt like a hundred. But I was right, too, and hefted it the way I would thousands in the years to come.

At my back, the woman said to Fenster, "That's an asset you've got there."

"Damn straight," I mumbled, following the man out to his car while she paid.

I filled out the proper forms. He hired me at minimum wage and a discount for any garden supplies I wanted to buy, and all the cold, bottled water I needed on the job.

"You won't regret this, I promise," I said.

"I already do," Fenster grumbled. "If you're done enjoying your break, I suggest you see Jones—he's the assistant manager—about doing some of the actual work you've been hired to do around here."

He worked me that first day. I'd sweated for years as the owner of Friday Harbor Garden Center, but I'd forgotten how much I'd toiled when I first started there in that other life and time.

I picked up my bottle of water and clocked out. My first day of work was over.

"See you tomorrow," I said.

Fenster waved. I walked out through the main doors, aware of the ache in my legs. Good old lactic acid. It would be worse in the morning. After a few days, the pain would subside as my body built muscle and grew used to the new demands expected of it. But the day's present drudgery was not yet over. I still had miles to go, just like in the Frost poem.

I cut across the rutted drive, turned onto South Main, and set off for my father's house. The woods thickened, blocking out all but splinters of early-evening sunlight. I trudged along the soft shoulder, exhausted but also satisfied by my accomplishment. First full day of time travel counterclockwise, and I'd already fixed one of the past's mistakes. I'd leapfrogged over the grocery store job I hated and gone right to the one that became my career and livelihood.

Time had been altered.

Forty minutes later, I reached the giant oak. My gaze lifted to its top, visible through a break in the canopy, its crown sipping sunlight. Closer, closer yet, I felt my expression tighten, my teeth grind, and my nostrils flare.

"You don't get him this time," I growled on my way past the murderous oak. "This time's gonna be different."

I came out of the conservation woods and picked up Dean Avenue. Steve's truck was parked in the Ranleys' driveway. How I wanted to turn left, pound up those steps, and ring the doorbell. But I was bedraggled, and the time wasn't right.

July 5. That's when Steve and I were fated to become a secret society of two. I was still a week early.

But when I turned up Juniper Road, I saw someone sitting on the front steps. My heart galloped. My breath hitched in my throat.

Wonder of wonders, it was Steve Ranley.

EX MARKS THE SPOT

Chapter 5

He was real. He was *here.*

I walked faster up the driveway. At first he didn't see me. When he did, Steve stood, and a wide smile broke on his face, replacing his scowl.

"*Steve,*" I sighed, his name the most powerful word to me, the pivotal ingredient in a spell that weaves magic.

He tucked his hands into the pockets of his jeans and balanced nervously on big feet in new sneakers—*no socks,* I again noted by the flash of bare ankles. A gray T bearing the logo of a major league baseball team and sunglasses raised to the top of his head completed his attire. He looked divine, perfect. Me, I was a sweaty mess.

"You're home," he said in that deep, manly voice.

In a way, I was. "Yeah."

We waited, neither of us saying anything at first. He smelled of soap, a man's brand, and clean sweat.

"Your dad said you were out, at work," he eventually said.

"Guilty. First day on the job. Everything all right?"

Again, he hesitated before answering. "Figured I'd take you up on that offer to hang out."

Chills raced up my bare legs. "Sure," I said. "But—"

"But?"

"I really need to shower."

"I can wait."

"Give me five minutes."

"Okay."

"Ten max, I swear."

He laughed. "Take your time, dude. I'm not going anywhere."

I unstuck from the spot and marched up the steps to the door. Partway inside the house, I whirled. "You want to come in? Have a cold drink?"

Steve laughed again, not at me, no. I sensed his relief despite his calm exterior. Like me, he was a wreck of nerves. "Go. Shower. I'll be here when you're done."

"You promise?" I asked and then felt foolish.

He fixed me with a look, once more in control.

"Okay, I'll be quick."

I nearly tripped over my own feet on my way into the house. I raced to my bedroom and its clown's wardrobe of options and pulled something together. Time seemed to drag out as I peeled off my work clothes and stepped under the hot spray. I scrubbed everything. I shampooed, toweled off, and brushed my teeth. The soap, shampoo, and toothpaste weren't the organic brands I'd insist upon using in future days, but they worked. With my heart lodged in my throat, I slapped on deodorant and pulled on clothes.

My pulse raced. My chest filled with anticipation. Reaching the front door took longer than it should have—what felt like a thousand steps instead of twenty.

I pushed open the screen door.

Steve was gone.

The joy soured in my gut. Over the course of the next several tense seconds, I contemplated if he'd ever really been there to begin with because, as I kept realizing, this was not how events had played out the first time.

Panic gripped me. "Steve?" I called.

I'd imagined the whole thing.

Then, from the corner of the garage, he appeared, cell phone pressed against his ear. Steve held up a pointer finger, urging me to wait, to stay quiet, while he finished his conversation. That allowed me to rein in my panic, catch my breath, and calm down. I sat on the top step and willed my pulse to slow.

"Yeah, later," I heard him say.

He killed the call but stood at the edge of the garage, staring at his cell for a few seconds longer. Then Steve walked over, and I was again struck by his lack of confidence. I remembered him always being in control. But that was an illusion crafted after the fact by time.

Steve moved beside me and sat. I caught his scent and grew intoxicated.

"You're here," he said, his voice like music I could listen to all day and night.

"Yeah, finally," I laughed. "You too. I'm so happy to see you."

He narrowed his eyes, but his smile returned. "You are?"

Oh, you have no idea how happy, I thought. *How much I've missed you. How I've traveled counterclockwise through time just to be with you again.* "Sure—I was getting pretty bored with it all too," I settled for instead.

Steve chuckled. I'd forgotten that sound and recalled how much I loved it. "This new job, what is it?"

I aimed my eyes down at his big feet and proudly declared, "Junior botanist at Friday Harbor Garden Center. It's a glorified title for wage slave, but it's a start. Gives me an opportunity to utilize all my knowledge about plants."

"That's great," Steve said.

"Yeah. And one day, I'll own the place."

His smile widened.

"You scoff now, but it's true. And when I do, that place will become something incredible. Not the rundown wreck it is today.

My garden center will be one of the mainstays of Friday Harbor, like the marina."

I sensed his gaze as he studied me, recording details in the growing darkness. I met his glance. Twilight had nearly surrendered to night, and yet I still saw the sapphire radiance in his eyes, their intensity robbing me of breath.

"What?" I asked.

Steve blinked. "It's just that . . . you know who you are. I'm jealous."

I remembered a similar conversation from that other time, on the 5th of July. The words were different, the meaning the same. "You know who you are, don't you?" I asked, mirroring what I'd said then when we were parked in his truck, shedding the last of our facades and, eventually, clothes.

Steve shrugged.

"You're Steve Lee Ranley," I said. "You played second base for the Friday Harbor High Schooners. You're going to the police academy in September."

"How do you know my middle name?" he asked.

Thinking fast, I answered, "Yearbook."

The truth was from a different time and series of events—one of those long summer nights together when I asked him everything because I wanted to know everything about him. The excuse worked.

"Honestly, I'm not sure about me," he said.

I sucked down air scented with Steve. "In what way?"

Our gazes met once more, and I saw his desperation. The words he longed to say refused to travel past his tongue.

"You can tell me. Tell me anything," I whispered.

"You're the only dude I know who's, you know . . . *gay*."

I tensed. I hadn't denied or hid that fact for years. I was comfortable in my own skin. That sudden tenseness owed to the fact that I was in unfamiliar skin, the me-who-was. But my mind was evolved. I ordered myself to relax.

"What makes you think I'm gay?" I laughed. "I mean, I could be straight . . . if not for the whole loving-the-penis thing."

Steve laughed too. This time the expression sounded like relief—relief that was badly needed.

"You have a girlfriend," I said.

"Yup."

"Lori O'Connor, right?"

The joy on his face flattened. Steve nodded. "For now. But I don't see us lasting much longer."

"Why?"

He hesitated. Our gazes held. "I think . . . I mean . . . I dunno; it's just that I have these feelings. I wish I didn't, but they're always there. How do you . . . ?"

"Become gay? Well, as I understand it, when the herd thins, we hang upside down in trees like vampire bats and wait for attractive men to come along. Then we swoop down, bite them on the neck—"

He laughed again, only it sounded sad. Boldly, I reached over and cupped Steve's face, loving the scrape of five o'clock shadow showing at just after eight at night. He leaned into my touch, half closed his eyes, and growled out his approval.

I whispered his name as I so often had into my pillow before and after his death in that other reality. His eyes opened, those magnificent twin sapphires, and he reached up, took my face in his big hands, and crushed our mouths together. The kiss was awkward, mildly painful, and more wonderful than any other I'd experienced. The taste of his lips overwhelmed me. He exhaled, and I inhaled his breath into my lungs. The hand I'd rested on his chest slipped lower, down to his knee. Unable to stop myself, I inched it closer to his crotch. My fingers gripped Steve's hardness through his jeans. Steve moaned his approval into my mouth.

55

The kiss continued. My emotions surged, crashing like the sound of waves that had greeted me back to this time and place. At one point, Steve tested my willingness with the tip of his tongue. I opened my mouth. His tongue darted in, his inexperience clear. I sucked on his tongue and continued to massage his erection. Steve moaned and pushed against my palm. His orgasm crescendoed, his gasps powered down, and his tongue slipped out of my mouth.

Steve rested his sweaty face against mine, his eyes shut, his smile there, dreamy, until the weight of what had happened sank in. Then his eyes shot open and he jerked away from me.

"I'm so sorry," he said.

"Don't be."

"But, *dude—!*"

He jumped up and adjusted himself. I saw that he was still hard in his jeans. I reached for Steve's hand before he stuck it down the front of his pants to shift things back into position.

"Steve, it's okay," I attempted.

"I gotta bounce," he said. "Later."

He pounded down the steps, got a few yards along the walkway, and stopped. I walked to the bottom of the steps. Steve backtracked and met me.

"Thanks," he said.

There was so much I wanted to tell him—about what had been, what was to come, and, mostly, how much I loved him.

"You don't have to thank me," I said. "I'm here for you if you need me, Steve. I'm right here."

He straightened, and his facade returned. Steve gently backhanded my stomach, and then gave me that tip of his chin. Saying nothing more, he turned and strutted away down Juniper Road until the night engulfed him somewhere on Dead Avenue, stealing him from my sight.

Electrified by what had happened, I tossed and turned all night, aroused and itchy all over. It hadn't played out the same in that other timeline, but a version of this night's events *had* taken place that July 5 when Steve picked me up on my long hike to Juniper Road after work. He nervously confessed to a level of confusion in his life and that he'd broken up with his girlfriend. We'd sat in front of my father's house in his truck, talking until he kissed me. In the wondrous confusion that followed, I touched his hardness. He'd climaxed. Then, embarrassed, he'd cut the night short.

"Those parts took place," I gasped at just after three in the morning. "But not the same way they happened here."

If there were common threads between Then and Now, Steve would come around after accepting the kiss, the touch, as being worth accepting in order to be happy. And he would be happy for those last two months of his life.

I masturbated, rolled over, and flipped sides again. The warm breeze spiriting into my bedroom smelled of summer's lingering heat. I loved him. I was in love again and at the start of that new love.

Guilt washed over me. Love? I was in love with my husband, Bradley. Only we hadn't met yet, and I told myself I had nothing to feel guilty about. At this point in my life, I was supposed to be in love with Steve Ranley.

And I was.

Tired, I rode beside my father. He dropped me off at the garden center. For the next ten hours, I labored, doing a hundred menial tasks that tested exhausted muscles but also established that I was where I belonged. At six, I hoofed it to Juniper Road along South Main Street, through the conservation woods, and past the Ranley house.

Steve's truck wasn't in the driveway.

Nor was it the next two nights I walked home from work.

It was July. I didn't wake up to find myself back behind the hybrid's wheel, as I'd expected. Behind the wheel, covered in broken windshield glass and soaked in blood, and thrust forward a decade into the future. But though Steve and I had connected earlier in this rewritten timeline than its predecessor, he hadn't come around for another visit. My worry built.

On my first day off from the garden center, I hung out in my room running through the things in the desk, closet, and under the captain's bed. I found the CD player, headphones, and the old case containing my music. I unzipped the case and scrolled through the offerings. I still had this case, this music, in the future.

My fingers slowed, stopped. I pulled out the CD. It was the debut from Muse, a well-loved favorite both Now and Then. Especially Then. It was also Bradley's favorite. I scanned the list of songs on the back cover.

"I Belong to You." That one was ours.

The strange sense of guilt and betrayal I'd suffered that night after Steve's visit was back. Why wasn't I trying to return to tomorrow, to him? I was so invested in fixing the past, I hadn't stopped to consider that I could be ruining the future. If I was successful— if I stopped Steve from dying—would Bradley and I ever meet?

I couldn't think about other parts of the bigger picture, only the one vital piece. I returned the CD to the case and pulled out Incubus. I slipped the CD into the player, donned my headphones, and turned up the volume. "Drive" poured out, haunting and appropriate, given my predicament.

Rapid thunderclaps sounded on the outside of my bedroom door, shocking me out of my reverie. I tore off the headphones.

"*Oliver*," my father barked.

"Yeah?"

"Phone," he said, that and nothing more.

I hopped off the bed. By the time I made it to the kitchen, my father was back behind his bedroom door, his role as head recluse secure.

The phone—was it Steve? I hurried over and picked up the receiver. "Hello?"

"Yo," a male voice I didn't recognize said.

"Who's this?"

The voice laughed. "Funny. What are you up to—besides basting your turkey?" More laugher followed, unpleasant on my ear.

I made the connection. It was Warren Rudd, one of my few high school friends from the summer following graduation, who wouldn't be a friend much longer if this timeline followed the other's course.

"Chilling. Listening to music," I said.

"Where the hell you been? I've been calling but no answer."

"Busy."

"Basting your turkey," Warren chuckled.

I exhaled. "I got a job. Hard work. Keeps me scarce. You'd know about jobs if you weren't so busy basting *your* turkey all the time."

"Ouch," Warren said. "You're mean."

"I gotta go," I said.

"Wait. My folks are throwing a cookout on the Fourth. Burgers, potato salad, that sort of shit. Can you make it?"

I remembered how cold Warren was to me the day I told him I was gay; how he'd walked away from being my friend without hesitation. "I'll let you know."

"What about tonight? You up for a movie?"

"I've got a date with my boyfriend. I'm gay, Warren," I said.

He chuckled again, the sound sharp. "Yeah, right—and I'm the pope."

"Goodbye, Your Grace," I said and hung up.

Chapter 6

At noon, I wandered outside to work in the garden. I pulled weeds, watered, and communed with the plants I'd nurtured from their start. There was something soothing about being out there, raking the soil, spreading fresh mulch. I hadn't lost my appreciation for and love of gardening in the life I knew a decade from my present point in time, but everything after August 30 of this year would be stained by an unwanted second shadow, one always there.

I pulled the lawnmower out of the garage, gave it a little maintenance, and started it up. The lawn wasn't particularly overgrown but would be by my next day off from work. I mowed up and down in a clean formation. On my way to the side of the yard, I saw my father, the recluse, standing on the front steps, studying my movements. I released the starter bar. The lawnmower died.

"Something wrong?" I asked.

"I was wondering the same thing. Usually, I have to threaten to evict you to get you do any yard work around here except your damned garden."

I shook my head. "Not a big deal, Dad. I'm just trying to help out."

I pulled the starter. The lawnmower chugged to life. I made my pass over the side yard and remembered how this facet of our relationship wouldn't change. We'd come to a kind of understanding, but closeness with us wasn't in the cards. He thought of Bradley as the son he'd always wanted. I wondered if the same would ever hold true with Steve Ranley if time could be altered and the two of us got the chance we'd previously been denied.

I finished mowing the lawn and felt somewhat Zen. My old life, which was really a new, future one, exerted its influence on my present situation. I thought about Blackberry Corners, and homesickness smothered my sense of peace. By the time I emerged from the shower, my mindset was focused again on this time and place.

Dressed in jeans and a clean shirt, fresh underwear and socks, and the same pair of kicks—first paycheck and I planned to buy new, comfortable sneakers—I sat on the front steps, inhaling the sweet fragrance of the lawn. I remembered about GLVs, green leaf volatiles. What my senses interpreted as a thing of beauty and comfort was really the lawn screaming out in agony, the smell of its blood and a chemical released as the individual blades of grass attempted to stop themselves from dying.

Way to kill a buzz, I thought.

I looked higher into cloudless sky the color of comfortable denim. Days and nights had passed, and I was still here. The script as I knew it hadn't played according to established scenes and scenarios. But it *was* real. Solid concrete, rough beneath my palms, composed the front steps of my father's house. The fragrance of green blood and the lactic acid ache in my calves weren't facets of a dream.

From somewhere in the neighborhood, the haunting music box melody of wind chimes played. I half closed my eyes, drew in a deep breath. Steve's handsome face materialized in my mind's eye. He was here, alive. All the days, hours, minutes, and seconds I'd wasted since my return to the past weighed down on me. I should have spent every moment with him, knowing the fate creeping closer in the very near future, now less than eight weeks away.

No, I would alter that outcome, cancel the tragedy. It was the only explanation as to why I'd been granted this second chance. A do-over. It had to be.

The chimes waned into the background, smothered by a truck's engine. I pulled my gaze down from the sky and tracked the sound to the corner. Steve's pickup turned onto Juniper Road. He pulled along the front of the yard and got out. T-shirt and shorts, sneakers but no socks, and one of those well-loved baseball caps that was a mess of frays around the bill from having been worn so often completed the image of his magnificence.

Our eyes met across the distance. He flashed the sparest smile. "You want to go for a ride?" he asked.

My insides ignited. I wanted to dance in place—the Cabbage Patch, the Floss, the Running Man, and the most outrageous show of pure joy possible—before sprinting to his side.

Choking down my urges, I calmly answered, "Sure, whatever," and stood. What felt like an hour later, I'd crossed the lawn and opened the passenger door, convinced that the heat inside would burn me alive.

My eyes recorded my surroundings, reacquainting with the truck's pale gray interior, the layout of the dashboard, the pine-scented air freshener, and the clean smell of Steve.

EX MARKS THE SPOT

Steve got in. Up close, I noted the hair on his lean, muscular legs; the scruff on his chin, cheeks, and throat; and the sparkle of those twin sapphires before he pulled on his shades, concealing them.

"How have you been?" I asked.

He nodded, started the truck, and drove up Juniper Road, picking up Old Coach. Wind streamed in through the open window, warm and heavy with the smells of summer.

"I'm happy to see you," I said.

"Good," Steve said.

"About the other night. What happened was okay, nothing to worry about."

He drove on, his eyes aimed at the road. It struck me that I didn't know where we were headed, not until he drove up to the gates of the cemetery.

"Uh, Steve," I said.

"It's cool. We can talk here and nobody will see or disturb us. Trust me," he said.

I began to tremble. Trust him? How could I tell him of the many visits I'd make to this place in the months and years ahead, first on foot during the winter following my shifts at the garden center and then over the course of a decade, driving here from Blackberry Corners when Bradley thought I was running errands.

He motored forward slowly, down the single-lane asphalt paths and toward the patch of empty green lawn in one corner of the cemetery that wouldn't remain empty for long. With my horror rising, I realized he planned to park his truck close to the actual place his grave would occupy if I were unsuccessful in altering the sequence of events leading up to August 30.

All heat fled my insides, and gooseflesh formed on my arms. I looked over at him right as we fell under the shadow of a tree. Steve turned away, a ghost beside me who was still alive.

"Stop, please," I said.

I reached over and set my hand on his bare right knee. The muscled, hairy flesh beneath my fingers and palm was warm, proof of life.

"Not here, Steve. Anywhere but here."

He looked over and studied me from behind his shades. "Okay, but where do you want to go?"

"Your place?" I suggested.

"No, my folks are home."

"I know a place."

It felt like one more betrayal heaped onto all the others when I'd visited Steve's grave under the pretense of buying milk or gassing up the hybrid. When you considered it, even my being here in this time was a knife driven into Bradley's back. I should have been home ten years into the future, with him at Blackberry Corners.

Ten minutes later, I was—after a fashion.

"Here?" Steve asked.

I pointed to the thin impression of a dirt driveway visible through overgrown sedge at the side of the road. He turned the wheel. His truck climbed the long drive and approached the abandoned bungalow house.

More shivers teased my flesh. It was the house as I remembered it at the start, before our loving restoration. Two windows were boarded over. The roof was a mess of old shingles, gaps showing in places, no shiny, indestructible metal. None of the plantings and gardens were there, only the dense woods brooding beyond the overgrown property line.

Still, its beauty filled me.

"Why this place?" Steve asked.

I buried my gaze in the trees and leaves undulating in the late-afternoon breeze. "Isn't it gorgeous?"

Steve laughed. "No, it's a dump."

"Don't you see the potential here?" I asked. "Some day, this house will be a showplace, and the grounds will be like a modern Eden. It has such promise."

"Yeah, to be flattened to the ground by a bulldozer," he said.

I turned away from the view, my heart, so full of love that I felt I'd come home, wounded over his words.

"Seriously, knock it down and put in something bigger," he said.

I was almost as horrified by his statement as I was his choice of hangouts in the cemetery. My mind, gifted with knowledge of the future, flashed back to the day Bradley and I first laid sight on the house and grounds.

"What do you think?" I'd asked, the skeptical one in our couple.

I could see how sure he was without his answer. The way his eyes sparkled and his mouth beamed in a smile despite the strict rule we'd agreed to follow in front of the Realtor.

"I think it's perfect," Bradley said. "It's the one."

"But are you sure? The place is falling down," I'd argued. "Are you sure you can fix it?"

"Pretty sure," he said, his enthusiasm unwavering. When I pressed him about specific details, he'd reminded me that he had the right tool for every job. Then he smacked my ass, not hiding that either from the Realtor's eyes.

And Bradley had been correct. He did an outstanding job of restoring the bungalow, as I had done in planting and tending the gardens surrounding our home set against the deep, vast woods.

Steve reached over and took my hand. I came out of the spell, but only partway.

"We aren't here to flip houses," he said.

I looked at him—so handsome, so important to me—and yet his words and nearness felt like an insult to our surroundings and to my husband in that other, future time. Calming, I squeezed Steve's hand.

"I'm sorry. I was wrong about being here," I said. "We should go."

"No," he said, leaning over, intending to kiss me.

I shrank away.

"What's wrong?"

"We can hang out at my father's house."

"Dude, won't your dad be there?"

I tipped a glance at the setting sun. "He's already passed out for the night by now. As long as we don't smash the place up too bad, we should be all right."

He remained where he was, expecting me to cave, to kiss him. But I didn't.

Not here.

He released me, circled the truck around the driveway that would one day shelter my hybrid and Bradley's wheels, and drove away. I watched the old, sad house fade in the rearview and wanted to tell it I'd be back, someday, to rescue it from neglect. But the promise felt insincere beside Steve Ranley.

When you own your own house and business before you've turned thirty, you forget what it's like to sneak around, hoping to avoid getting noticed.

Steve switched off the ignition, flashed me a confident smirk, visible in the glow of the nearest streetlight, and nodded. I nodded in return and got out, my heart beating frantically. We sneaked across the lawn, through the front door, and along the dark house to my room. I welcomed him in and closed the door. Before I'd even switched on the bedside lamp, Steve took me in his arms. I nestled

EX MARKS THE SPOT

into his embrace, aware of his warm breath near my ear, the scent of his skin, and his hardness pressing against mine.

He grunted out something that made no sense but was easy to translate. I turned my mouth toward his. This time, our kiss was more uniform though just as tense as its predecessor.

Steve's arm tightened against my lower back. I mumbled something equally cryptic around his lips, kissed harder, and extended my right hand lower over the firm, high perfection of his sports-sculpted ass.

In the darkness, it was easy to believe I was still being haunted by a phantom.

"I missed you," I said after our mouths parted. "Oh, how I've missed you."

"Yeah?" he asked, his word a challenge. "Why's that?"

There was so much I wanted to tell him. But before I could, Steve took my hand and guided it off his ass and between his legs. I ached to profess my love, a love that had survived tragedy and conquered the laws of space and time. Steve only cared about sex.

I reached my other hand toward the wall and located the light switch. The lamp beside my bed dispelled the darkness. Steve drank in his surroundings, moved to the bed, and sat.

"Now turn it off," he said.

"Why?"

He pulled off his baseball cap and T-shirt and then kicked off his sneakers, baring those incredibly sexy feet. "Hurry up, would you?"

I'd have given him anything at that point.

Darkness once more engulfed us.

A light breeze stirred the scarlet curtains and whispered into the room in a disembodied voice. As the night deepened, I pressed against Steve's bare body, aware of our sweat and his lingering taste. In the hour following our arrival, I'd reacquainted myself with the topography of his physique. More than through the rings of trees, worshipping him from head to toe—especially Steve's toes—had brought me back in time. I recalled details clearly, as well as the reasons I'd fallen so completely for the young athlete—soon-to-be rookie cop—who'd taken me to my bed.

"That was great," he said, breaking the silence.

I leaned back into him, the firmness of his muscles, the scrape of hair from the leg cast over mine, solidifying what I felt. Love—the kind that was so hungry it would consume you to live without it.

"Glad you liked it. Me too."

I reached for his big hand, the one he used to throw a baseball and pleasure himself, and laced my fingers between his. I brought our joined hands to my mouth and kissed the back of his.

"You're different now," he said.

"I am?"

"Different than when we were in school."

My eyes searched the shadows. "How so?"

"I dunno," he sighed. "More mature, maybe. More with it. It's like you know what to do, what to say, at all times."

"Is that a compliment?"

"Totally," he said. "It's like you're still Oliver Canfield, but a different one who's got a few extra minutes head start on the rest of us. Me, anyway."

I sucked down a breath that smelled of our sweat and sex. "I am."

Steve went quiet again. I rolled over, an awkward move that made the captain's bed creak beneath us. My eyes had adjusted to the darkness enough for me to see the face of the living ghost sharing the bed with me.

"I am different—because of you," I said.

He studied me in return, not commenting at first. The air thickened in my imagination. Gravity doubled in weight. All of the reasons that had led to this moment, the secrets and mysteries, inched closer to my tongue. I had to tell him the truth. I would.

"What about me?" Steve asked.

Ice formed over my skin. In the shadows of my old bedroom, I made out the sapphire color of Steve's eyes locked on me without blinking.

"Steve, on South Main Street, headed into town," I said, my voice not much louder than a whisper.

"What about it?"

"Do you know that giant red oak tree, the one on the right-hand side after the road dips?"

"Oak tree?" he asked.

I readied to tell him what had happened in that other time. All of it.

Chapter 7

The words raced up my throat—*car crash, that evil bloodthirsty oak, a decade of suffering on the heels of the argument between you and your father . . .*

But before anything emerged, the scarlet curtains billowed like an omen, a visitation by spirits, and on the breeze was the smell of a storm. The first drops of rain pelted the backyard. Thunder rumbled in the distance.

"*Dude,*" Steve said, bringing me back to the moment. "You were saying—?"

How could I share with him the knowledge of his death now, weeks before it had happened in that other time? Anything I said on the subject would make me sound crazy and likely drive Steve not only from my bed but my life. It was too soon to go there, despite my wanting to so badly.

"It's just that," I said, laughing an insane little laugh. "You should know, if you don't already, that I had the biggest crush on you throughout school."

I laughed again. Steve's eyes remained focused on me. Outside, the world lit. Several long seconds passed before the thunderclap caught up to the lightning.

"What's that got to do with some oak tree on South Main?" he asked.

"I was just thinking out loud. You know, more of that useless plant knowledge that fills my brain," I said lightly. "Did I tell you that one day I'm gonna own that garden center? It'll be the crux of my own little business empire."

He exhaled a chuckle. "That dump of a garden center and that wreck of an old house. Some empire."

I stared at him, again wounded by his words. Even at our lowest points, Bradley had never mocked my dreams. The next flash of lightning illuminated the room in fluorescent white. In its after-glow, I fumed.

"What?" Steve said, a defensive note clear in his tone.

"I'd never make fun of what's important to you," I said.

He sighed again, unhooked from me, and sat up. Naked, his feet on the floor, he slumped forward. "Sorry."

I didn't remember any of this side of him, likely because it had never been given the opportunity to show itself the first time around. Then, I wasn't the me I had become in the decade that followed this summer. There'd been no Blackberry Corners. I hadn't been hired at the garden center until Christmas of that year. I'd messed with the events of time as I knew them. Was I so naive or stupid to think there wouldn't be consequences for my actions?

"Look, I didn't mean to piss you off," he said.

I choked down my hurt and waved it away. "I'm not."

Outside, the storm opened up, deafening for the first dozen or so seconds of its furious cascade. I set a hand on Steve's bare spine. He quivered beneath my touch before turning to face me.

"Why?" he asked.

"Why aren't I pissed?"

"No. Why the crush on me?"

I considered my answer. "Look at you—you're so hot, so manly, so *magnificent* that the Greek gods must be jealous."

He said nothing, just stared at me.

"You in your baseball uniform," I said, all nerves and clutching at reasons. "I mean, *seriously!* You know how straight guys say 'Think about baseball' when they're trying to remove a sexy image from their brains? Even straight dudes couldn't do that if they were thinking about you in your Schooners uniform, especially with the long socks and stirrups. And, man oh man, speaking of which . . . those legs of yours!"

"My legs?"

"Long, hairy—hairy legs on a hot baseball player—and if I haven't told you this or shown it by the way I sucked on your toes, you have the handsomest feet."

Steve chuckled. "They're feet—there's nothing attractive about them."

I set my hand over his. "You're a rugged, masculine athlete. Your feet are amazing."

"You're funny," he said, though the comment didn't sound as insulting to my ear as his digs at the garden center and the abandoned house that would become Blackberry Corners.

"My feet, my legs, and my baseball uniform," he said. "That's it? Those are the only reasons?"

I sat up and positioned myself beside him on the edge of the bed, naked in terms of both body and soul. Outside, the rain's cadence continued, steady but now more subdued.

"No, there's more," I said.

But to tell him more would mean revealing knowledge learned out of time. I offered nonspecifics, hoping they'd be enough.

"You have a big heart. I know that heart's confused right now, trying to figure out stuff. But it will, and I know you'd be there for me if I needed you, like a hero. A white knight."

He rested a hand on my knee. "She said something like that the other day."

She—I did the math.

Steve sucked down a breath. "I told you about my girlfriend, Lori."
I nodded.

"The other day, that phone call I made while you were shower-ing. I decided it was time to break up with her."

"Did you?"

He shook his head. "Not yet. But, yeah, I'm confused all right."

I wrapped my arm around his naked back. "Are you gay? Bisexual?"

"I don't know what I am, who I am. Only that . . ." The sentence went unfinished.

Steve bridged the short distance between us and kissed me. I kissed him back. My right hand reached between his spread legs. He was once more erect.

Only that what we're doing feels good, my inner voice filled in the missing words.

I lowered between his legs, took his thickness between my lips, and proved again how much I loved him, even if I couldn't exactly explain why beyond the physical reasons. While down there, loving our connection, I, too, wondered about the love part.

For the first time, beyond my attraction for him, I couldn't really explain what I'd loved about Steve. Asked the same question about Bradley Steven MacIntyre, and I could offer up a hundred reasons why on the spot—

First Christmas, the box full of movie DVDs, all of them my favorites. It wasn't the gift but the fact that he knew me so well.

How he sent me flowers every August 30—not the morbid, funeral kind, but always a dozen roses, bright and fragrant.

The pomegranate accent wall. That had been my idea, but he'd honored it. And in our little home office, the first objects to enter after the furniture were my grandfather's bronze horses, because Bradley knew how important they were to me.

The list was endless.

With Steve, there'd been no instances outside of sex and kissing I could point to. I told myself it was because our time together was so short. He'd died before we could make any memories of substance other than physical ones.

His grip on the back of my head tightened. I drove away all thoughts except for bringing him to climax. The rain fell, and we made something like love, further rewriting the events of a history that now existed only inside my head.

The rain let up by midnight and the storm took an interlude. I walked with Steve out to his truck. The air smelled of fresh rain and mowed lawn. After our night together, I was giddy but contained my excitement.

"What did you tell her?" I asked.

"Lori? That I wasn't sure. My folks are having a cookout on the Fourth. She's supposed to come over, but . . . I don't know."

"You'll figure it out by then," I said. "I know you will."

And I did, at least as much as what I recalled from established history. Steve pecked a kiss crookedly on my mouth, where I imagined him tasting the dregs of his own nectar, a kind of mark of ownership.

"Tomorrow?" he asked.

"I'm working until six."

He pulled his keys out of his shorts pocket. "I'll pick you up after your shift."

"Okay," I said.

He got in and drove down Juniper Road, turning left onto Dean Avenue. An emotion I hadn't experienced in years filled me, that sense of anticipation for birthdays and Christmases from youth only stronger because I was now an adult and the looming event was another night with Steve.

I waited for at least a minute before returning to the house and cuddling atop the bunched bedclothes that smelled of our love.

My father dropped me off on his way to the marina and, as usual, few words were spoken. I was sore from physical work and sexual pleasure but took to my shift with enthusiasm, something not lost on my boss.

"You're in a happy mood," Jim Fenster carped.

"I have a lot to be happy about."

"I hate happy before eleven in the morning," he said. "So how about you try to be as miserable as the rest of us?"

"Whatever you want, Boss," I said.

"I feel the same way about ass kissing as I do that happy-clappy shit before eleven."

I carried the stack of clay pots out to their new destination, as instructed. "Yes, sir—I promise not to kiss your bony ass until after eleven, *sir!*"

Fenster laughed. "You've got a mouth on you. Now *that* I can respect."

You and Steve, I thought, and then I had one of those think-of-baseball moments. Luckily, when I envisioned Steve Ranley in his blue-and-white Schooners home uniform, the trick canceled out thoughts of Jim Fenster.

After eleven, Fenster called me aside. We convened under a willow tree whose giant root ball was encased in burlap—the sort of end-of-season castoff I'd have loved to take home to plant beside the brook.

"You want some extra hours?" he asked.

"Sure," I said, before remembering my secret date with Steve. And it *was* a date, one he'd arranged. "As long as it's not tonight. I've got plans."

"It's tonight—we're open for three extra hours because of the holiday."

"I can't," I said.

Fenster's ugly side, the bully persona he often degenerated into when he didn't get his way, took over.

"Look, kid—I'll admit that I've been impressed with you. You're a hard worker. I like that. But I'd like it more and likely remember it at the end of the season when I have to lay off people if you'd help me out when I ask. You know, what's it your generation says? If you do me a solid."

"Fine," I said. "But you owe me."

"No, I don't," he said.

I had to hand it to him. Fenster had finally removed the smile from my face.

I hadn't known the specifics of the night's date, other than it would likely involve more kissing, more sex. It struck me that now, as in that other reality, Steve and I weren't so much a couple as friends with benefits. That thought darkened my mood almost as much as Fenster's twist of the arm to get me to stay late on this of all days. But then I remembered how fantastic those benefits were. On the surface, Steve Ranley was way out of my league. Fate had

EX MARKS THE SPOT

brought us together twice now in two timelines, and though the
fit wasn't exactly perfect, it felt fairly damn excellent. Friends with
bennies? I could live with it.

For more than a week, I'd subsisted on peanut butter sandwiches
brought from home. Fenster sprang for pizza, and I helped myself
to two slices of pepperoni and mushroom before glaring at the
clock—it was almost six.

"Back in a flash," I said, hastening out through the main building
and into the humid early night beyond.

Steve's truck was parked in the center's lot, impossible to
miss. I hurried over to the open driver's side window. He sat behind
the wheel, shades over those magnificent twin sapphire eyes, a stony
facade fixed in place.

"Hey," I said.

"You ready? Hop in."

For a second, I considered risking Jim Fenster's newfound faith
in me and leaving with Steve. At this time in my life in that other
reality, I might have. But here, I had foresight into the future, a
future I'd already tampered with.

"I can't," I said.

"Why not?"

"The boss asked me to work three extra hours tonight. And by
'asked,' I mean he gave me no choice. Even threatened. If you
were an officer now, I'd have you arrest him on charges of general
assholery and having a face like a sour grapefruit."

My attempt at humor fell flat. "Are you serious?" Steve asked.

"I'm afraid so. But I'll be done at nine—can you come back in a
few hours and we can start the party later than planned?"

The smile was back on my face, only this time I sensed its desperation.

"Three hours," Steve sighed. "I'll try, dude."

It was clear that he wasn't happy. I shared his disappointment,
and a sinking sensation seized hold of my insides.

78

"Please?" I asked.

He leaned forward and started up the truck. "Sure."

Saying nothing more, he drove away. His answer did little to alleviate the growing malaise within me. I turned back in the direction of the nursery and, off and on for the next three hours, assisted customers and attended to the garden center's needs without being told what to do, going instead on instinct and memory.

At nine, I clocked out. I exited into the muggy darkness, worried that Steve wouldn't be there. He wasn't.

"You need a lift home?" Fenster asked.

I shook my head. "Thanks, no. My ride's probably on his way."

Fenster considered me for another moment. "Good work, Canfield. I'd almost say it's great, but I don't want you thinking you're important around here."

"No worries there," I said, flashing a counterfeit smile. I waved. He drove away.

I stood in the parking lot waiting for the telltale flash of approaching pickup truck headlights. I was tired, sore, and sweaty after a long day's work. But I waited for what felt even longer, and when Steve Ranley didn't return, I started the walk back to my father's house.

The woods brooded around me, dark and foreboding. The few cars that passed me on South Main offered an illusion of hope that was never realized. None of them were Steve.

Night birds sang. My imagination wandered, hastening my steps. Eventually I neared the place in the road where, on this side, it ascended to Dean Avenue. I was close to the bloodthirsty oak.

Around me, the night fell silent, as though the world was holding its breath. I walked on, tracking the oak's location through wide-open eyes.

The road leveled. I came out of the cathedral of trees and crossed onto Dean Avenue. To my left, the Ranley house sat in darkness except for the light cast by the living room television. Steve's truck was parked in the driveway. As I continued past, my heart so wounded I wanted to cry, I remembered yet another reason I loved Bradley.

Though I'd done it to him by returning here, not once had my husband ever left me stranded.

Chapter 8

I did my best not to think of it as a betrayal, but over the next day and the morning of the Fourth, my stomach churned and my resentment deepened. Steve never showed, and as I stared at the bedroom wall, things about him I didn't care for during our counterclockwise reunion festered.

A knock sounded at my bedroom door.

"*Yo*," I called.

"You planning to see your grandmother today?" my father asked through the closed door.

I sat up. "Grandma?"

"Barbecue at your aunt's house. If you want to ride over with me, have your butt ready to go by eleven."

"Okay," I said, dazed.

I hadn't thought about the rest of the Canfield clan. Since my return, Steve had consumed me. It was only Steve. The reality check added to my malaise. Of course Steve Ranley would be my sole focus. It was why I'd traveled back in time—to rescue him.

Hacked off at him as I was, I couldn't lose sight of that goal, my raison d'être. Even so, the chance to see my grandmother, Louise Canfield, got me moving. I showered, selected something half decent from my peasant's wardrobe, and did my best to choke down my rising nerves over a family reunion I hadn't planned for.

"How's work?" my father asked.

I stared out the window, feeling lost and haunted. The world raced past as we traveled out of Friday Harbor for the town of Gray, New Hampshire, whence our family hailed.

"Demanding," I said. "Back breaking, but fulfilling."

My father drew an audible breath. "I think it's been good for you. I'm proud of you for sticking with it."

His praise shocked me. "I plan to stick with it for the rest of my life. It's a job now, but one day it'll be my career as well. More than just a livelihood."

"That's the right attitude. Don't screw it up."

There it was, the expected dig. I looked at him from the cut of my eye. In typical Lawrence Canfield fashion, he couldn't offer a compliment without adding an insult.

"I'm not going to screw it up. Trust me," I fired back, my tone clear.

"You so sure about that?"

No matter what, he'd get the last word. I swallowed down my response, which started with a resounding "*Yes—!*" I was sure. So sure that not only would I not screw things up, I'd own that garden center and transform it into something great. It'd become as big a draw in town as his lousy marina, a feat I wouldn't have accomplished bagging groceries at Victory Supermarket. *Victory*—it was anything but during the short time I'd worked there. And what a stupid name for a grocery store chain, I'd always thought and still did in the ten years after this moment. Victory over what? High prices? Locally grown produce? Nothing in their fruit and vegetable section matched the organic fare I harvested from the gardens at Blackberry Corners.

Today was the Fourth, tomorrow the fifth day of July, the life-altering date in the other timeline. Thoughts about my father's veiled insult dissolved. Those regarding Victory Supermarket and the role it had played on July 5 persisted. We arrived to Gray and my Aunt Lucy's house and, for the second time, I stepped back through history.

It was all how I remembered—the in-ground pool, the long folding tables covered in checked cloths and platters of food, the big umbrellas, and red, white, and blue balloons tethered to shiny strings and tied to the privacy fence. Cousins I hadn't spoken to in years, aunts and uncles, and especially my grandmother Louise were all present.

I approached the table where she sat, a small though regal woman in a pastel pistachio sundress, hat, and sunglasses. Emotion almost as intense as what I'd experienced at seeing one soul raised from the dead filled me for another. I walked in what felt like slow motion.

"Grammy?" I said.

Louise's face lit. "Oliver!"

I leaned down and we embraced. She smacked a kiss to my cheek and I relived a hundred memories at the same time, all of them triggered by the fragrance of her rose hand cream.

"You look so good," she said.

I knelt beside her, taking in her beauty. My voice hitched with a sob. "You too, Grammy. More beautiful than anyone on Earth."

She cupped my cheek. "I'm so happy to see you."

I nodded. Tears flooded my eyes despite my best efforts to stop them.

"Get yourselves something to eat," my Aunt Lucy said. She was dressed in a colorful one-piece bathing suit, her hair a wild perm of curls. "I cook it—but I don't wait on anyone."

I hugged my grandmother again and didn't want to let go.

Burgers, dogs, and barbecued chicken roasted on the grill. Potato salad, macaroni salad, and salad-salad accompanied, along with watermelon, icy soda, and my Aunt Lucy's signature Fourth of July dessert, a white sheet cake decorated in fresh strawberries for the stripes of the flag and blueberries for the stars.

I talked with cousins, aunts, and uncles, but mostly it was chit-chat about the new job and future plans now that I'd graduated. My father and I held to a comfortable distance from each other. The younger cousins and the kids from the older set of my generation frolicked in the pool. Sunshine beat down on this snapshot glimpsed out of time—in a few short years, all of this would wane following my grandmother's death. Family gatherings of this scope would lessen, shrink, and end altogether.

Looking over, I saw my grandmother sitting alone. I got up from the lawn chair my butt occupied and moved beside her at the table.

"You're back," she said.

The words struck me as eerily prophetic, more powerful than she'd intended them. "I am."

She took my hand. We faced one another. I trembled.

"What's wrong, Oliver?" she asked.

In a low voice, I confessed. "I'm confused. I'm not exactly sure what I'm supposed to be doing, just that I'm determined to make things right."

She studied me from behind her sunglasses. "You will," she said. "And don't worry. Not one bit, Oliver. You'll find him. He's out there."

"Him?"

"The one you're supposed to be with. The one you'll fall in love with and spend the rest of your life with, happy and safe in that love. You know how I know? Because you're my wonderful grandson, and you deserve nothing less!"

I didn't deny her words. It was my first coming out apart from with Steve, and it was easier than I could have imagined.

The next day at work, July 5, I went about my duties both inspired by my talk with my grandmother and anxious about the significance of this turning point in my life.

After lunch, while walking delivery invoices to Jonesy, the man I would soon replace, I caught a hint of movement from the corner of my eye. When I turned toward it, I saw a woman who looked familiar, though not as she was the last time I was with her.

"Crazy Plant Lady alert," Jonesy chuckled beneath his breath.

It was Ms. Burch, looking only slightly less crazy ten years back in time.

A chill engulfed me. I handed Jonesy the invoices. "I'll take care of her."

Jonesy snickered. "You need your stash refilled or something?"

"Or something," I said and pursued.

Her hair wasn't as long or silver. She wore a light summer top with a floral print and a denim skirt. The way she carried herself, however, hinted at the version to come. She moved with a kind of stealth, her body rigid, her eyes scanning.

"Ms. Burch?" I called.

She stopped and stood with her back to me. "Yes?"

"I wanted to say hello. Oliver Canfield—I had you for Sophomore Biology two years ago."

She turned and flashed an untrusting little smile. "I remember you."

"You were an inspiration."

"Was I?"

"I've always had a green thumb. Love plants, trees—all flora, really. Fascinated by their mysteries. Do you have a minute?"

She tipped a look around. "I'm not sure I have the time. I'm very busy today."

"Please, it's important—a scientific matter related to the plant kingdom, and you're the only expert on the subject I know."

She faced me. "What's your quandary?"

"The rings of trees. Do you think there's any significance to them apart from representing a year of new growth?"

Her demeanor changed, softened. "That is a very good and, frankly, intriguing question, Mr. Canfield."

"The idea and answer haunt me," I said.

She considered my words. "Why?"

"Do you think it's conceivable that a person could somehow travel back through time using the apparatus of those rings to unleash their energy the same way nuclear fission works—by smashing through and tapping the release? And if he or she could, would they be able to affect change in an already determined timeline?"

Her eyes widened. "I'm not a physicist."

"No, but you are a biologist, someone who knows the animal kingdom and the plant kingdom thoroughly."

A smile spread across her lips, and it looked crazier than anything I'd seen in her expression throughout either reality. "Intriguing! I never would have considered this theory before."

"Maybe you will—in some future dream."

She came out of her trance. "Let me ponder this some more and get back to you. Will you be here?"

I laughed. "At the garden center? For ages yet to come, I imagine."

She resumed her slink through the main building to the greenhouse, only to stop and turn back to me.

"As far as the second facet of your question, I'm not sure. We think of time as rigid—events already having happened unable to be undone due to some frame of order, some bigger power at work. But if, supposing the first equation is possible—time travel—one would have to factor in some give-and-take."

"Give-and-take?" I repeated.

"Yes, that the time traveler, having traveled back through time in the release of that cosmic energy, would be permitted some level of freedom of motion to instill changes. But think of those changes as ripples on the water, spreading out in concentric circles. Little echoes. Each of those ripples widens, covering more surface. Each change to the timeline would have a corresponding outcome, an alteration—some with consequences."

Her words chased me for the rest of the day. I'd already committed changes to the timeline—I'd hooked up with Steve earlier than in the first performance of my life, what I was beginning to think of as a dress rehearsal. I'd come out to my grandmother. And instead of the lousy summer job at the grocery store, I'd taken a position at the garden center six months ahead of the original schedule.

Victory Supermarket. I was supposed to be there on this night. My mind raced. I would have gotten out of there at six, if memory served me. Which meant I'd be walking home between six and seven when Steve picked me up at the side of the road, and we spent the long night parked in his truck in front of my father's house talking then kissing then . . .

At a quarter to six, I clocked out early, telling Fenster I'd make up for it the following day.

"You sure as shit will," he grumbled.

I hotfooted it down Harbor Road to North Main Street, passing the cafes, the bank where this version of the garden center and its future incarnation both did business, and hurried on through the parking lot. Victory Supermarket was the place where people from Friday Harbor and three surrounding towns did their grocery shopping. The place looked packed. My flesh grew itchy at the memory of my first shift here, a memory that now only existed in a timeline that couldn't be trusted.

Ripples on the surface. Ms. Burch's words pursued me into the store. Maybe this loose reenactment of all that came before would lessen the ripple effect.

The automatic doors whisked open, discharging a gust of cool, dry air. I passed from the July humidity outside into the air-conditioned chill. A quick glance at the clock above the line of grocery carts revealed that I'd made the journey with five minutes to spare. In that other timeline, I would still be among the ranks of unfortunates working at the ends of conveyor belts, delicately placing eggs and bread on the tops of grocery bags.

I continued past into the store. I was hot and thirsty. I had a few dollars in my wallet—money I'd assumed was left over from graduation. Four minutes. I wandered down the aisles to kill time. At the back of the store, adjacent to the deli and cases that held multicolored parfait was another that contained premade sandwiches and bottles of cold soda and seltzer water. Most of the store's workers flocked there for lunch breaks. I chose a bottle of seltzer with raspberry and lime and was intending to continue to the register and out for the long walk back to Juniper Road to test if Steve would pick me up when *he* walked past.

Maybe it was the chill in the air, the cold bottle of seltzer in my grip, or something *other*. The shiver tumbled down my spine. After it finished and the world stabilized, I saw a young man checking me out from the periphery. I turned to face him. He wore board shorts and flip-flops and a T-shirt that hugged a long, impressive torso. His sunglasses were perched on his head. He wore his hair short, and a thin, trimmed beard and mustache on his handsome face. He smelled like coconuts from suntan lotion and clean, male summer sweat.

"*Bradley*," I gasped, unable to contain my surprise.

The younger version of my future husband straightened, shifted the shopping basket in his fingers from one hand to the other, and fixed me with a look through narrowed eyes. "Do I know you?"

"What are you doing here?" I asked. Another shudder tumbled down my backbone. "It's too soon—we don't meet for another two years!"

He glanced around, laughing nervously. "Uh . . . *what?*"

In the next second or two, I drank in his image. He still owned those shorts. I didn't recognize the T-shirt. He'd replaced those flip-flops a few summers before with new ones. His athlete's legs were as attractive as I remembered, his arms as strong. Though younger, he was the man I'd married, the one I loved after Steve Ranley.

"Sorry," I said, gathering myself. "I thought I knew you."

"From the marina?"

"Marina?"

"Yea, we've got a boat there. Look, I'm not sure what's happening here . . ."

Neither was I. Bradley's family *had* summered in Friday Harbor and used the marina the year we met. And as sure as he was my Bradley, my future husband, I was just as certain that he'd been checking me out when I saw him staring.

"My name's Oliver," I said. "Oliver Canfield."

"Bradley MacIntyre," he said.

He extended his free hand. I took it and a circuit was completed, one in which energy was exchanged along with silent understanding.

"Great to meet you, Oliver," he said.

I held on, thoughts about my fated July 5th ride with Steve completely forgotten.

Chapter 9

How often in the years to come would his hand hold me, comfort me, show me that I was respected and loved? I gazed into Bradley's brown eyes. They weren't as striking as Steve Ranley's sapphire blues, but in them was a depth and sincerity unmatched by any other man's.

"So you're from around here?" he asked.

"Friday Harbor lifer," I said. "You're just visiting?"

"New Jersey, up here for the summer," he said.

Of course I already knew most of the details of his life. How, for instance, one of his baby photos captured him throwing a tantrum on a picnic blanket because the family's beagle had licked his face. He hated salad until he started eating the fresh produce from our very own garden, after which he declared that he could taste the sunlight on the tomatoes. A million other things, the significant and the mundane, his whole history already existed inside me.

"My dad manages the marina," I said.

"Larry?"

I nodded.

"He's a cool dude," Bradley said.

I laughed. "He's cool, all right. Like a blizzard." Even now, at the beginning, my father and Bradley were chums.

While we stood there posturing and the clock ticked forward, it struck me that the younger version of my future husband was still checking me out. Of course he was—I knew he was attracted to me by the history I alone was conscious of. There didn't need to be any awkward moments or anxious questions. He liked what he saw, and I sure did as well. In ten years, Bradley would be handsome and athletic. He was in this time, only younger, and that hint of naivety added to his attractiveness.

Bradley smiled, flashing a length of clean white teeth, the gesture as charming now as it would be then. "So what's there to do in this town besides hanging out on boats at the marina?"

"Not much, I'm afraid. I drown out the threat of boredom by working as much as possible."

"Do you? What kind of work?"

"I'm a slave over at the garden center. But someday, I plan to own the place, which means I'll have to work twice as hard. Yay me!"

He laughed. "Very good." Then Bradley fidgeted. "Hey, I got no plans except for this."

He shook the shopping basket, which contained a large sub and two cans of cold soda. "I know it's crazy to ask . . ."

"Dinner? I'd love that."

Relief washed over his face. "Really? I mean, it's crazy right, me asking you? You're a stranger to me, I'm a stranger to you—"

"I already said yes, Bradley. Besides, we're not really strangers," I said.

"We aren't?"

Oh, the reasons I could have offered him. "No, you know my dad, remember?"

"That's right."

I led the way to the register. There, mirroring a million shopping trips to this same place in the decade to follow, I unloaded his shopping basket and handed him the few bills in my wallet.

"For my half of dinner," I said.

He paid. The bagger who wasn't me started to shuffle our purchases into a plastic shopping bag.

"*No,*" we both said at the same time. "*I hate plastic bags.*" That, too, came out in unison.

We eyed each other, smiled, and picked up our peasant's meal. Then, together, we walked out of Victory Supermarket. It sure felt like a victory.

I didn't recognize the car, a newer model with yellow Jersey plates. "It's a rental," he said. "Just for the summer."

It was nice. Not as nice as the truck he drove in the decade after now, but I appreciated the traces of Bradley I saw among the unfamiliar—a baseball cap, a dog-eared paperback novel sitting atop a beach towel, CD cases in the catchall, and the St. Christopher's medallion hanging off the rearview mirror. That same religious artifact would grace his truck's rearview in the future.

I sat in the bottled heat. Bradley started the car. Like me, I knew he wasn't a fan of air-conditioning. He thumbed the button that opened his window.

"I can put on the AC if you prefer," he said.

I shook my head and opened my window. "This is better."

Bradley smiled again. "So, where should we go to enjoy our dinner? The garden center? The marina?"

"No," I said. "I know the perfect place. On your way out of the parking lot, turn right."

I instructed him where to go. Our surroundings grew more bucolic.

"How do I know you're not an ax murderer leading me to my death?" Bradley asked, that crooked smile showing, his eyes hidden by shades.

"You don't. But I'm not, and you'll get that by the end of dinner. Besides, I prefer a garden trowel to an ax, and I'm pretty sure you can hold your own."

"Was that a compliment?" Bradley asked.

"Oh, most definitely."

"Okay, how do you know that I'm not an ax murderer?"

Again, there were so many reasons I could give. "I'm a great judge of character."

At the turnoff, I pointed the way. Bradley drove his rental up through the overgrown sedge, and once again I found myself gazing at the future site of what would become Blackberry Corners. Bradley drove right to the same spot that would one day be his parking place, shut off the ignition, and studied the old, sad house.

"Cool," he said.

Butterflies flocked in my belly. "Don't you think this place is wonderful?"

He studied the neglected little bungalow before commenting. "I think it's got great potential."

"You do?"

He nodded, not breaking focus with the house. "You don't know this, but I'm a hell of a handyman."

I did know it, but I kept my secret. "Are you?"

"Sure. I grew up in a hardware store. I can do just about anything—construction, plumbing, light electrical, even roofing. I could turn this place from an abandoned wreck into a showplace, like that."

He snapped his fingers. Then he turned to face me.

"I have this dream about living here when it's a showplace," I said. "Transforming the grounds around it into gardens—flowers, ornamentals, fruit orchards, and especially blackberry bushes. The heritage kind."

He smiled. "Why blackberries?"

"They're sort of my favorite."

Bradley's smile persisted. "It's a nice dream. If I had it, I wouldn't want to wake up."

Suddenly, I wanted to cry. "I don't know why I ever did."

His gaze stayed on me, no doubt trying to decipher this stranger and his cryptic answers. "Is something wrong?"

"No. In fact, for the first time in a while, everything feels right."

Not commenting, Bradley reached for our dinner. He handed me the sweating bottle of seltzer from one of the cup holder's two slots and unwrapped the sandwich.

"Hope you like Italian," he said.

"I'd like liver if it was with you."

He snorted. "That's an odd thing to say."

"Why? I despise liver."

"That's why it's strange. I hate liver, too. In fact, I'm—"

"—never going to eat it again," I said, finishing his sentence.

Even two years before we were supposed to meet, that was just the way we rolled.

Windows open, the sultry breeze stirring around us, Bradley handed me half the submarine sandwich. It smelled of oregano, pickles, cheese, and green peppers. My stomach grumbled. I was hungrier than I thought.

"So you're going to own the garden center and this house, which will be a showplace—a phoenix rising from the ashes. I like it," he said.

"Maybe there's enough room in that dream for you."

It was a bold thing to say, but I already knew the outcome if it followed the tracks of known history.

"Me?"

"If you're interested."

"Hey, it's just a sandwich, not a gold band."

I took a bite and rolled my eyes. "It's the best sandwich ever."

Still grinning, he lifted the top and picked out the green peppers and slices of tomato.

"What are you doing? That's the best part," I admonished.

"Not a fan," Bradley said, offering me the castoffs.

I took them, added them to my half. I'd work on his resistance to salad things later, no doubt. For now, I was just so happy to be with him.

"So what about you?" I asked.

"What about me?"

"Dreams, plans?"

He shrugged, looked out the window at the little abandoned bungalow, and swallowed down the mouthful of food. "It's kind of like yours."

"Do you believe in fate, in destiny?"

Bradley turned back in my direction. His gaze tightened on me. "I believe you're the strangest dude I've ever met. But I like strange."

We both laughed. He leaned over. I met him halfway. Briefly, our lips connected. Though short, that little kiss filled me with light and energy. Bradley pulled back, his face flushed but his smile still there.

"Bradley," I sighed.

The sound of a phone singing a standard riff of outdated music shattered the moment. Bradley reached into his shorts pocket and pulled out his cell.

"Yeah," he said. "Just eating a bite for dinner."

The conversation wasn't much longer than our kiss.

"I'll be there as soon as I'm finished. Bye."

He ended the call and pocketed his phone.

"Problem?"

"No, not really. Clingy family wondering where I am, that's all."

I finished my sandwich and washed down the last bite with a good pull of bubble-water. I didn't want our time together to end, but soon it would.

"Can I drop you somewhere?" Bradley asked.

"My father's house."

He brushed the crumbs off his hands and started the car. "Goodbye, little house and future blackberry patch," he said, and we drove off.

"This is the place."

He looked at my father's house. "Nice, but I like that last one better. Has its own unique charm."

"Me too, and I agree," I said, aware of the wide smile on my face.

"Bradley, this was wonderful. The best first date in all of human history."

"Date?" he chuckled. "What makes you think this was a date? Do you think I'm into other dudes?"

I laughed too. "The kiss, the deep conversation, the instant connection—I'd call it one hell of a date."

"So does that mean you're up for a second one?"

I looked into his eyes, still shaded by his sunglasses despite the day's crossing into twilight, and nodded. "I guarantee it."

We remained that way for untimed seconds, gazing into each other's eyes, surrounded by the deepening purple of day's end. Bradley blinked first, but only to reach into the catchall for a pen. He scrambled to find something to write on. I extended my arm.

"Seriously?" he asked.

"Never more serious, babe."

"*Babe,*" he repeated. "I like that."

He wrote his phone number on the palm of my left hand. The point of the pen tickled, and more of those giddy little icy-hot pinpricks crackled over my skin. When he was done, I admired his artistry.

"Let me guess—you're thinking you'll never wash that hand again."

"Close. I'm thinking that the hot young man sitting beside me writes in Egyptian hieroglyphs."

I leaned over. We kissed again. This was right. This was home. I stepped out of Bradley's ride and waved goodbye. He lowered his shades, taking a good stare and clearly liking what he saw given that he licked his lips on the drive away from my father's house. To my delight, at the end of Juniper Road before it met Dean Avenue, he pulled a U-ey and drove back up for a second look. I waved again. He continued toward Old Coach, back in the direction from which he'd come.

My insides felt full of sunshine. I stared after him for a few more seconds before continuing into the house, where my father was waiting to crush my joy.

"Who was that?" he demanded.

I didn't care for his tone. "Someone you know, a guy named Bradley MacIntyre. His family's here for the summer. They've got a boat down at the marina."

He scowled. "What were you doing with him?"

Not that it was any of his business, I wondered if he'd seen our kiss made under cover of the nascent twilight. "We were just hanging out. Aren't you happy that I'm making friends?"

My father snorted in response. "Seems like you have enough already. Warren's called for you twice, and the Ranley boy was at the door earlier, looking for you."

I absorbed his words. Warren Rudd wasn't important to me—knowing what I did about his treatment of me in the other timeline, I'd decided to cut off the friendship early. It was no great loss. But I'd been so consumed over being with Bradley that I'd overlooked the significance of this day. I was meant to take a ride home with Steve after clocking out at the grocery store. Instead, I'd met the man I'd one day marry and had ridden home with him. Ms. Burch's words about ripples in the fabric of time and such consequences as yet unknown played through my memory with an ominous echo.

"Okay, now you know," my father said and headed back to his room, closing the door behind him.

Fresh sweat broke out all over my body. I hadn't realized I'd clenched my hands into fists during my father's interrogation.

"Oh, shit," I huffed.

I opened the left. Most of Bradley's artwork was gone, the numbers bled out of cohesion by sweat.

I told myself it didn't matter—he knew where I worked and lived, and I knew his family was in town at the marina. We'd find our way back to each other, as we had earlier in this timeline than the one already established. My focus shifted to Steve Ranley, who had visited the front door while I was out with Bradley. I could guess what he wanted from me, and that idea conflicted with the intense emotion so fresh and reassuring over being with Bradley.

In a daze, I showered and dressed in fresh T-shirt, socks, and underwear. Lounging on my bed with the TV muted, my mind wandered. I'd implemented changes to the flow of time, unleashing those aforementioned ripples. As far as I could tell, there was no exit strategy—I couldn't just up and leave, go back to what was or had been. No heel clicks would transport me home as they'd done for Dorothy in *The Wizard of Oz*. I could only inch forward toward August 30, the pivotal date, one tick of the clock at a time. On that day, maybe time would reset.

The scarlet curtains stirred. A low, ghostly moan whispered into the room. Then his voice called to me.

"Oliver, you in there?" Steve asked. "Oliver, I need you. Need you bad, dude!"

Chapter 10

I moved through the dark house to the front door, my pulse throbbing. For those twenty or so steps, I waged a secret, silent war from within the confines of my psyche. I loved Bradley. Everything told me we belonged together. But I also loved Steve—lusted after his body, was enamored over his memory, at least—and now, in this time, I was supposed to be with him, not Bradley.

I opened the door and he stormed in, taking me into his arms before I could move out of the way. We remained in that position, me tense, him smelling of fresh sweat, pine, and a hint of beer on his breath. Worries that my father might catch us faded as I warmed to his touch.

"I'm glad you're here," he whispered at my ear before kissing the side of my face.

I nodded. "Good to be with you. Come on."

I led the way to my bedroom, a place we both wanted to go according to my brief contact with the full tent between his legs. But Steve held onto my wrist and drew me back.

"Wait—you got any beer?"

"I don't drink. Hate the stuff."

He held on. "Does your dad?"

My father kept a few bottles in the fridge, mostly for the end of the day and weekends. Not sure why, I nodded and headed into the kitchen. I'd catch hell if discovered, so I'd have to get away with it, I decided. I pulled one longneck from the bottom shelf and resumed course to my bedroom. Steve followed.

Inside, the TV cast its ghostly glow on my night visitor, clad in loose-fit black or navy cotton shorts, sexy kicks minus socks, an old white T, and his favorite baseball cap. I desired him as much as I wanted to be with Bradley. One reason owed to hormones—I was eighteen in body, older in soul—and the other to history. Hormones, in this instance, were poised to win the conflict.

I handed Steve the beer. He cracked off the cap and took a deep pull, the kind that would have left me passed out on the floor. He remained standing.

"I did it," he said after muffling a belch.

"It?"

"I broke up with her. Lori. My girlfriend."

Just like in that other timeline. "Steve," I said.

"I went to the nursery to tell you and drive you home, but you weren't there," he continued.

I dissected the information. "Did you drive past Victory Super-market on the way back?"

Steve took another swig and then answered. "Why would I go that way—we live in the opposite direction."

So that, too, had changed. If I hadn't taken a lift home with Bradley, I'd have walked the long way to Juniper Road on foot, my fated meeting with Steve erased from this reality. Because that pivotal event had taken place earlier and under different circumstances.

Because things were different and becoming more so, becoming jumbled. Ripples in time. Little was certain.

"I did it," he repeated. "Aren't you proud of me?"

"Very," I said.

I moved toward him. He set his beer on the desk and met me the rest of the way, seizing my face in his big hands, cold and damp from the bottle, and crushing our mouths together. His lips were sweet from the beer, which fueled my arousal. After that first kiss, clothes came off along with fears. More of our private sexual intrigue was promised to mark the night, replacing what had happened in his truck during that other timeline's sequence.

"Where were you?" he asked.

The tone of the bed's other occupant suggested something I hadn't expected or prepared for—ownership of a kind. He was out of his relationship with Lori O'Connor and had done that, in effect, for me. Telling him I'd spent the afternoon and early evening with the younger version of the man I'd one day marry wasn't an option.

"I told you. I was at Victory."

"Why?"

"For something to drink and eat," I said calmly. Funny, how easy lying about my actions and motivations had become since traveling counterclockwise through time. "I work long, hard hours at the garden center. If you'd driven past, you would have seen me walking along the side of the road."

That part was true, at least in the other timeline.

His hand, resting on my shoulder, drew away. Steve narrowed his eyes on me. The temperature in the room plummeted before surging up to what felt twice its earlier heat. I shifted, aware of the sweat.

"What?" I asked.

"There are times, I dunno, I feel like you aren't telling me every-thing. That you know more."

I forced my gaze to meet his. "That's because I do. Somehow, I've got a sense of it all. The bigger picture."

"Mind letting me in on some of it?"

I forced down a heavy swallow and nearly gagged on the dryness in my mouth. "I know this summer has been and will be the best of our lives. You and I, we'll give each other joy that will echo into the future."

The room fell silent apart from Steve's exhale as he listened to my explanation.

"But the summer will end, and what happens after the 30th of August . . . that's yet to be seen."

"When you talk like that, you seriously freak me out," Steve said. "Like I told you, you're different now than when we were in school."

"I've matured," I said.

"Five minutes into the future. It still freaks me out."

"And, apparently, makes you hard," I chuckled, given an out that would end his interrogation.

I walked my fingers lower, between his legs, and gripped his thickness. So Steve Ranley considered us a couple now—or at least that I was his. That part hadn't come for weeks down the line in that other history. The morning we ate wild blackberries for breakfast after spending the night in his room. Oh, I still knew the details intimately.

Steve dressed by the light of the TV. I watched, aching from the love that was made and also aching for more, hungry for him due to the forbidden knowledge I alone possessed. From beyond the window, the melody of the neighbor's wind chimes played. Their melancholy song drove home a warning about the track I was on. What if I saved Steve? That was my goal. What if I stopped him from dying against the trunk of the monstrous oak on August 30? And, in accomplishing that, he and I ended up together rather than the life I knew with Bradley?

For the first time, the possibility struck me, crashing over my soul like the thunderous waves that had greeted my return to this time and place. Those ripples on the water that the Crazy Plant Lady had talked about, those consequences for having screwed around with time, cast a chill over my flesh.

"What's wrong?" Steve asked.

"Nothing."

"Come on, you're lying," he said.

I sucked down a breath. The air in my room smelled of sweat and sex between men. "I just got cold, really cold, for a moment," I said, and that was the truth.

He bridged the short distance between us and took me back in his arms. A life with Steve Ranley—I'd wondered of that very outcome before and especially after his death. It wouldn't lead to a life at Blackberry Corners. But it also wouldn't end in a cemetery burial plot.

Steve lowered his forehead against mine. "I have to go. Tomorrow night?"

I closed my eyes, savored our connection for all the time I could, and nodded. "Sure. Hey, tomorrow's payday. Maybe we can do something."

He slapped my ass. "That's what I plan to do," he said, his confidence restored, his cockiness back. "I'll pick you up at six."

"Be on time," I said.

I walked him out to the front door. Carefully, I added the empty bottle to the recycling bin under the kitchen sink. There was no way my father would think I'd taken one of his precious beers.

Back in my room, I fell atop the sweaty bedclothes. Sleep instantly claimed me.

"Did you take one of my beers?" my father asked.

"No—hello, have we met? You know I hate that yeast urine."

He grumbled under his breath and turned the key in the ignition.

While backing out of the garage, he muttered something that sounded like he wished I had—beer instead of that girly seltzer water I was always drinking. He drove me to the garden center. I got out and thanked him. I marched in through the front door ready to start my shift.

It was the usual backbreaking list of demands. I unloaded and moved supplies from a delivery truck mostly without any help, assisted customers with orders, and, though not asked to, pushed a broom around the front of the place and through the main building, a habit I'd picked up when I became the manager and one I'd honor as the owner.

At eleven, Fenster tracked me outside to the thinning selection of ornamentals not yet claimed for the season, which I was watering and rearranging for maximum appeal.

"Nice touch," he said. "I like the ambition I'm seeing out of you."

He carried a business-size envelope, which he handed to me.

"What's this?"

"Your weekly insult. Only you get it every other week. Don't spend it all in one place."

I accepted the envelope and opened it. Inside was the familiar green payroll check. I'd put in more than eighty hours in my first two weeks. A decent chunk was gone to taxes, but what remained was more than enough for new sneakers, a phone, maybe a haircut with money left over to sock aside.

At lunch, I rode with Jonesy to Harbor Bank and cashed my check. I put half the money in my wallet, the rest back in the same envelope and tucked it into the pocket of my cargo shorts.

A life with Steve. I'd already lived through the fears of being married to a police uniform, that any routine traffic stop could end in gunshots fired and crippling loss. As for loss, I'd already lost Steve once. I knew what it was to be gripped by crushing grief and to spend whole days in bed without eating, showering, or talking.

My thoughts drifted back to Bradley and our unexpected date held two full years before we were meant to meet. While watering flats of marigolds, I acknowledged how right we were together, the perfect fit. He and I would restore our little house and live mostly happy lives there. Happy apart from the long shadow cast over us by the phantom of Steve Ranley.

I turned off the hose and another deluge took over. Tears spilled down my cheeks. The pungent fragrance of the marigolds added to the raw emotion holding me in its grip. I remembered the flowers I'd given to Ms. Burch, the ones that reminded me of the Mexican Day of the Dead. Wiping my eyes, I attempted to compose myself. When that failed, I put down the hose and retreated to the staff bathroom, where I ran water and splashed my face. Eventually the tears stopped.

Feeling like I was making some progress in both life and mission, I clocked out at six. Steve waited for me behind the wheel of his pickup. I was his, according to his own language and actions. He'd chosen me over his girlfriend. Doing my best to hide my happiness, I walked to the passenger's side and got in.

"Hey, you," I said.

Steve stopped fiddling with his phone and looked over. His face was a mask from which all but the barest trace of emotion had been ironed away. A game face—the kind hockey players and baseball gods show on the day of a big matchup. His shades hid his eyes. Only the slight, cocky hint of a smirk at the corner of his mouth showed through his veneer.

"'Sup," he said and started the ignition.

The truck's engine rumbled to life. I understood that I was seeing the public face of Steve Ranley, the one he would show to the outside world whenever we were together. With Bradley, we were a couple whether at home or dining at a favorite restaurant or cafe like Happily Ever Apple, which served the best apple tarts. We shopped together, hit the hardware store and movie theater as partners first and then husbands. We'd never projected false faces and had even shown public affection when appropriate.

"Where do you want to go?" he asked, breaking the chain of my thoughts.

"Shoe store, phone store, and then dinner on me anywhere you want."

While I shopped, Steve waited in his truck in the parking lot. I tried on new sneakers without a second opinion, another of those small future joys I'd know with Bradley. I bought two new pairs of kicks, both far more comfortable than the old ones that tormented my feet. I bought my first cell phone and signed up for a basic monthly plan. At one of the walk-in hair places, I got my mop shampooed and chopped, again without feedback.

When I returned to Steve's truck, he eyed me with suspicion. "What did you do to your hair?"

What I'd done was get the style I'd wear in the future, and one that mirrored his current athlete's cut. "Don't you like it?"

"No," Steve said. "I liked it the way it was. This . . . it's like I'm looking in a mirror."

I swallowed my disappointment. "Don't worry, it'll grow out quickly. Before two weeks are up, it'll wrap itself around my neck and threaten to strangle me if I even think about chopping it off."

I laughed. He didn't. I showed him my new sneakers. He said they were nice. With my phone, I told him the first number I'd call and save was his. He flashed an unconvincing smile and drove to the diner, where we ate burgers and fries and drank cold soft drinks, but he didn't show much in the way of conversation.

Certainly nothing to indicate we were anything more than friends, anything at all like a real couple.

The following morning, I handed my father the envelope containing four hundred dollars.

"What's this?" he asked, that usual sharp edge of distrust in his voice.

"Open it up."

He did.

"Room and board, Dad."

He reacted with surprise, at first saying nothing. "I haven't asked for room and board."

"Not in so many words, no. I'm trying to be responsible. I don't expect a free ride living under your roof."

My father attempted to hand the money back. "Keep it. I'd rather you save up for a car and your own place."

"Already working on those," I said. "The money's yours. I'll have another for you at the start of next month."

His attitude softened. "Thanks. It pleases me to see you working so hard at something you love."

"When you love it, it doesn't always feel like work," I said, which was true.

We didn't talk any more than the other times on the drive to the garden center, but, like some other facets in this do-over of the timeline, I sensed I'd made progress in my relationship with my father.

My day was barely an hour along when Fenster stuck his face into the back lot and shouted my name.

"Canfield, you have a guest," he barked. "You know my rule about socializing on the job!"

I shot him my middle finger. "When he buys a thousand bucks worth of merch, you can thank me by kissing this."

Fenster said, "You wish," and vanished back inside.

I trudged through the succession of buildings to the front, thinking it must be Steve or maybe Warren Rudd, the latter come to darken my mood. But no, standing there in flip-flops, shorts, a T-shirt, and the most radiant smile in all of human history was Bradley Steven MacIntyre.

Chapter 11

"*Bradley!*" I said.

Joy radiated in my expression. There was no use trying to mask it, so I didn't.

"Miss me?" he asked. I nodded. "Funny, 'cause I figured if you did, you would have called by now."

I flashed the palm of my left hand. "I sweated off the number, I swear."

I pulled out my new cell phone and told him to repeat his 4-1-1. As he spoke, I dialed his cell. Bradley's phone rang. He answered it.

"Now I have you programmed in and you have mine. End of problem," I said into the phone.

Smirking, Bradley said into his cell, "I like the new haircut. Suits you better than that shaggy look. I can see more of your beautiful face."

My smile widened. "You think so?" I asked the voice at the other end of the call while standing less than a yard from the caller.

"I do," Bradley said, mirroring the most important words he would say to me in about six and a half years' time on the day we were legally married.

We stared at each other, put down our phones, and savored a moment that required no words until Fenster entered from the door to the greenhouse.

"About that tree—juniper, was it?" I asked loud enough for my boss to hear. "This way."

I waved for Bradley to follow me out to the yard where the ornamentals were lined up thanks to yours truly. He played the game with me.

"Yes, a juniper—that's what I came here looking for," he called out, making sure Fenster heard his words too.

Electricity crackled over my body. I was so happy to see him, to be with him, that everything felt fresh and new because it was. Granted, this was a different scenario than our first courtship, but knowing all I did, I was confident things would turn out well.

"I had to see you," Bradley said, now in a voice meant only for me. "I couldn't stop thinking about the other night, about you. July 5 will always be with me."

I tried to ignore the significance of his words even as, shielded from view by a wall of flowering shrubs, I turned, reached for Bradley, and fell into his arms. Our lips met, their alignment perfect, and we kissed.

"Me too," I said once we parted. "It's almost like we were meant to be together."

He beamed while studying my face. "I thought the same thing. It's freaky how I feel like I already know you. Groovy, too."

"Maybe you do. And who says 'groovy' anymore?"

Bradley laughed. "See, I knew you were gonna call me out on that. That's what I mean. Freaky. *Groovy.*"

I smiled. "Very groovy, babe."

"I like the haircut. A lot."

There it was, more proof that Bradley and I were the perfect fit that Steve and I never would be. Warmth filled me. Bradley, so close, smelled of suntan lotion and clean sweat. I wanted to kiss him again—more, to make love with him as we'd done so often in our relationship. Most of all, I desired his nearness.

"Have dinner with me tonight," he said.

"A second date?"

"Sure."

"Of course. *Yes*," I said.

He lowered his shades, a measure of satisfaction crossing his handsome face. But it wasn't confident, certainly not cocky. That wasn't Bradley's style.

"When do they release you back into the wild?" he asked.

"Six."

"I'll be here at five of," he said, and I knew that he could be trusted. Bradley had never, would never, leave me stranded.

"It's a date. Now, about that juniper tree," I said.

"Wait, that was real?" He gave me a look, laughed, and purchased a beauty for just under twenty bucks, which I lugged out to the trunk of his rental.

Right on time, Bradley waited to collect me. I clocked out and resisted the urge to skip to his car. I got in, loving my surroundings. Loving *him*.

"Good to see you," I said.

"Great to be seen."

He clapped a hand onto my bare knee and drove out of the lot, his other hand on the steering wheel. For the first time in a long while, I had no worries. The reprieve was brief when, mere seconds after traveling away from the Friday Harbor Garden Center, we passed Steve's truck. I tensed.

"What's wrong?" Bradley asked.

I tracked the black pickup until it turned into the garden center's lot. My first instinct was to tell Bradley to turn around, to take me back. But then I saw that it was six minutes past the hour.

"Nothing," I said.

I'd pay for the night's sins in the morning.

We drove to Azure Cafe, one of the town's favored destinations for both locals and tourists. The cafe offered alfresco dining on a flower-lined patio with stunning views of the harbor. With the sun sinking behind the trees and a sultry breeze stirring across the lake, the setting was romantic, ideal.

"It's not a premade sub from the grocery store," Bradley said after we were seated at a bistro table for two beneath a large umbrella.

"I loved our first meal together," I said.

He leaned forward. I heard the nervous tap of his feet beneath the table as he wondered what to say next.

"You're not worried about us being seen together in public?" I whispered.

Bradley shook his head. "Should I?"

"You, me—on a date?"

His expression darkened. "Now that you mention it, yeah, I'm worried . . . that some other dude will see you and try to steal you away from me."

I chuckled. He smiled. Our waiter brought us glasses of ice water with wedges of lemon. He set our menus down and promised to come back to take our orders.

Bradley scowled, this time the look sincere. "So, do you mind my asking if there's someone else?"

I sipped my water while considering my answer. "There's a friend. His name's Steve."

"Steve? Or *Steven*—I'm a 'Steven,' you know. Middle name."

Oh, I knew. "Steve. He's in trouble. I'm trying to help him out of it."

Bradley absorbed my confession. "Are you and he serious? You know, *boyfriends*?"

That term hadn't ever been used, so I answered, "No."

114

"So you're available?"

"Maybe—for a special guy. A groovy one. What about you?"

Bradley leaned back. "I've had both—boyfriends and girl-friends. Nothing special, though. Haven't met anyone who fits the description."

"Until now."

"We'll see," he said.

He ordered a steak and fries. I said to make it a double order and asked for a salad. The meal came out, and my mouth watered.

"Want some of my salad?" I teased.

Bradley growled like a bear and dug into his steak.

"Let me guess—you love to barbecue, right?"

He admitted he did, and I remembered all our times at Blackberry Corners gathered around the grill.

"What else do you know about me?" he asked.

Grinning to myself, I stabbed at the beet greens and endive in my salad. "That you're an incredibly kind soul. You're always there for your friends and family. You have excellent taste in music—and in the bedroom, I'd guess you're quite aggressive."

"Want to find out?"

I nodded. "Eventually."

"Oh? When?"

"Fifth date. Fourth if I can't wait."

"Waiter, *check please*," he called out, clearly not caring who heard or was wise to the fact that the two of us were on a date.

"I got you something," Bradley said. "It isn't a bouquet of flowers. That's too expected, so I went bigger."

He popped the trunk. The juniper tree was still inside, where I'd loaded it hours earlier.

"Poor thing," I said.

"Hey, it needs a loving home, and since I'm like half a day's drive from New Jersey, I thought . . . how about your place?"

"You mean my dad's."

"You guys do live on Juniper Road, so it kind of fits. Unless you want us to plant it near that little house."

I faced Bradley. This all seemed so familiar, so correct, even though it occurred out of synch with the established timeline.

"Juniper Road's fine," I said.

Bradley smiled. "I've been thinking about that other house, what I'd do there. Start at the foundation and work my way up. New roof. Metal, I think. Something that will last and stand the test of time."

"The test of time," I repeated.

We got into the car. Bradley started the engine and again reached over, placing his hand on my knee. I shuddered, loving his touch, his scent, everything about him.

"I think I remember the way back," he said.

I reached down and set my hand atop the one on my knee. "Me too."

At one point he released me, but only to turn on the radio. He coaxed the CD hanging out of the player into the tray and advanced the selection to a later track. Muse's "I Belong to You" poured out at a decent volume.

My next breath came with difficulty. It was the song we'd danced to at our wedding, the one I most associated with us as a couple.

"You said I had great taste in music," he said above the slightly sad melody.

"The best," I said, my voice hitching with a sob.

Warm air streamed through the windows. His hand returned to my knee, and I decided, there and then, that I belonged to him and he to me.

We belonged to each other. That was how fate meant for us to live.

I would still stop Steve from driving on the ominous date looming closer. But I had made my choice, and I wanted to go back to the life Bradley and I had built together—me, owning the garden center, him among Friday Harbor's finest, and the love we knew at our Blackberry Corners.

In front of my father's house, Bradley shut off the ignition. We sat in darkness broken only by the nearest streetlamp. I heard him swallow, a dry and nervous sound. My heart raced.

"So," he said.

I leaned over and met his kiss. I caressed the side of his face, loving the familiar scratch of his beard. He playfully raked his fingers through my hair. In the other timeline, Bradley had loved the way I cut my hair. I hadn't changed it or allowed my mop to grow out since.

He grabbed my hand and kissed my palm, the tickle of his beard scintillating, erotic. So much so that I boldly allowed my hand to drop to his abdomen. From there, it was a short distance to the prize. Bradley was as erect as I was. But after a few fumbles, he shook out of the spell, breaking our lip-lock.

"Whoa," he said. "What about the fifth date and all that jazz?"

I chuckled again. "'All that jazz'? I thought 'groovy' was a blast from the past."

He captured my hand again and pulled it off his hardness. I wasn't offended, only disappointed. I'd never desired him more than at that moment.

"You know, it's worth saying that the hunt is just as important as the catch," he said, his voice sounding so dry that I imagined his mouth had desiccated to desert.

I kissed him again, tasting his nerves. "You're worth waiting for."

Bradley flashed a proud smile. "You think so?"

I nodded. "I know so. Okay, we're up to the third date as of this moment. As soon as we knock the next one off and the one after that, I hate to break it to you, babe, but the hunt is donesies and we're gonna consummate this very sexy and quite wonderful new relationship of ours."

He kissed me harder, hungrier. With very little effort, I imagined him climaxing without so much as being touched. I knew Bradley Steven MacIntyre—even before I was supposed to.

I pulled away and cupped his face. "This hypothetical next date . . . ?"

"I have family plans tomorrow night."

"Isn't it a bit early to introduce me?"

A serious look crossed his face. "Uh, I meant—"

"Relax, I was joking. Beside, tomorrow night after work I have to plant a juniper tree."

He softened. "Right after that, I'm free."

"It's a date. What do you want to do? The movies? I bet we'd have fun at the cinema."

"No, I want to talk," he said quickly, and I instantly understood that he'd thought about the answer, which was classic Bradley.

"Talk?"

"You and I, just talk. Ask questions. We tell each other everything, because I want to know all about you and I want you to learn everything there is to know about me."

My memory, with its powers of second sight into a time I was no longer sure was even real, flashed back to a similar "date" I'd had during that other summer with Steve, a night in which I'd asked him all those details of his life and history like his middle name. In retrospect, that occasion had been one-sided. What Bradley offered me was a chance to ask and be asked, this time the game of curiosity shared by both participants.

"That sounds like one of the best dates possible," I said.

Bradley answered with a nervous laugh. "Don't be so sure. You don't know about my baggage."

Oh, but I did. Bradley's amounted to the equivalent of one small carry-on tote not big enough to be checked as luggage. It struck me that in being honest, my baggage could fill one of those 18-wheeler moving trucks, because in a full disclosure situation, I'd have to share my knowledge of the future.

The heat sitting on top of my flesh turned clammy. "I'm game," I said.

"You working that day?"

I nodded.

"I'll pick you up after your shift. Don't worry about dinner—I'll bring something special, you'll see."

I guessed what he meant. In the past, using what had become our unique couple's language, I translated that Bradley would arrive with a kind of picnic meal. Cheese—usually Swiss—crackers, grapes or strawberries, and cold drinks; some of our best meals together were little picnics in the living room or bed in front of the TV.

My face serious, I said, "It sounds wonderful. I can't wait."

I kissed him again. Then, slipping from the car, I lugged the juniper tree out of the trunk. He'd been wrong about the flowers. In that other time, he would never forget to present me with them every August 30, like clockwork.

I planted the juniper tree after work in a corner of the front walk, right where it would face the road, which only seemed fitting. On that hot afternoon, the juniper's pungent smell struck me as sort of sexy, something to be associated with Bradley. I watered it

EX MARKS THE SPOT

thoroughly, returned the shovel to the garage and the hose to its rolled-up holder, and showered. No sign of Steve Ranley marked that night.

I crawled into my bed, smelling him on the sheets. I would wash then on my next day off from the job. I would enjoy Bradley's company tomorrow night after work. We'd enjoy a picnic—our first in this new reality. I fell asleep feeling happy and hopeful.

And then I had the nightmare of all nightmares.

Chapter 12

I walked through a dense fog, conscious of the pain in my bare soles as I traveled over ground, rocks, and sharp twigs. In a daze, I continued forward, half aware of my surroundings, which looked to be woods out of focus cloaked in night and drapes of gray. It was warm out, damp from humidity. Still, my body felt encased in invisible ice. I walked on.

My inner voice asked, *What are you doing here?*

I attempted to respond, only my lips refused to cooperate. So I thought the words instead. *You mean here, as in this time in the past?*

Yes, in the greater picture's sense. But I mean here, as in now, right now. I'm dreaming?

No, sorry.

I asked the voice to clarify, but it chose that moment to pull the silent treatment on me. Not dreaming? There was no chance I was awake. My last conscious memory was of passing out in my bed, excited for my upcoming reveal-all picnic date with Bradley.

The chill surrounding me deepened, helped along by a gust of breeze that stirred the clouds of fog and scattered raindrops clinging to leaves. I froze where I stood and gazed ahead into the darkness. The indistinct phantoms of the nightmare forest stabilized, and I found myself staring at the thick trunk of a gigantic tree. A low, throaty moan slipped past my sleep-frozen lips. It was the oak, the murderer. Fear ignited in my stomach.

I remained unable to move, thinking for another second that this had to be a dream. It couldn't be real. I hadn't walked out of the house in the night, drawn here of all places. At the exact instant, my inner voice chose to break its silence—

No, Oliver, you were summoned!

Something slithered or skittered over the top of my bare foot, shocking me the rest of the way awake. I jolted out of the fugue state, aware that I was sleepwalking.

I'd walked out of the house and into the conservation woods, just like the night in the future when I made it all the way to the dry brook at Blackberry Corners and saw the blood.

Summoned? By whom or what?

I forced my eyes higher, up into the fog-choked branches at the murderous tree's crown.

"*You*," I spat.

For a moment, I expected an answer, perhaps from whatever demon inhabited the oak's numerous rings. Hell had rings too, according to Dante. But the oak didn't need to respond with words. It had deigned to offer up proof of its power. I had tampered with time. It would not be denied the feast of blood it demanded on August 30 and had made its warning clear.

Terror rippled over my skin. My teeth chattered. I willed my frozen legs to thaw and took a step away in retreat, half expecting the tree to reach down and grab hold of me with one of its clawed branches, wielding it like an octopus tentacle.

"You won't win," I spat, taking another step. "I'll stop you. I'll save him. You can't have Steve Ranley this time. You can't!"

I whirled, unconvinced of that promise hurled into the universe despite my shouts, which echoed through the night woods and up into the foggy sky. At first, nothing but shadows met my eyes. Panic tried to seize control of my dazed mind. It didn't help that I also noticed that I was wearing exactly what I had on when I'd crawled into bed—a T-shirt and tight, white underwear, nothing more.

One lone, distant star appeared in the eclipse. I blinked and realized it was a streetlamp on Dean Avenue. That landmark helped me reestablish the lay of the land. Shaking all over, my teeth continued to chatter; with a rising sense of panic, I saw that my surroundings had lightened. The day was dawning. The sound of a car door closing reached across the woods. The world was waking up, and I stood out in the open dressed only in my underwear.

There was no way I'd make it back to my father's house on Juniper Road unseen, so I went the only place I could.

Steve's house.

The fragrance hit me—sweet, comforting, even sensual. On the last leg out of the conservation woods, I'd come across the blackberry patch where, in that other reality, Steve and I'd enjoyed a unique breakfast after sneaking out of his room at dawn. I dug in my soles and glanced around. The brambles were as I remembered them, covered with jewels of fruit only starting to ripen. Again I returned to Ms. Burch's words about ripples and consequences. In this timeline, that morning memory wasn't likely to play out.

I crept up to the wood line and peered around me. The sky had gone from black to gray, the last vestige of night before sunrise. A quick mental calculation put the time close to five in the morning. I couldn't see any signs of activity in the upstairs windows of the Ranley house.

Steve's bedroom was downstairs, directly off the brick patio. He'd moved there when he was thirteen because he needed privacy. I knew this from the other timeline and the few nights I stayed over at his place when his parents took weekend trips throughout what remained of that lost summer.

The melancholy song of wind chimes played from somewhere nearby in the neighborhood. I crept out of hiding and made my way through the backyard, around the hulk of the old car Mister Ranley was always working on to restore, lawn furniture, and to the screen door, beyond which Steve's bedroom awaited. The grayness was almost gone. Sunlight glowed beyond the barrier of trees.

"*Steve*," I whispered into the house.

The inside door was open, the room still bathed in shadows.

I called his name again, this time louder, the panic in my voice clear. Movement stirred. I heard the groan of a mattress, the scuffle of bare soles across laminate floor, and then a gray ghost appeared. Steve was dead, a specter, according to the vision. I'd failed to save him from the fate I'd traveled back in time to undo.

"Dude, what are you doing here?" the sleepy ghost asked.

He reached for the door handle. Sunlight illuminated the healthy color of living flesh on his hand and arm. Steve opened the door. I hurried inside.

"Are you nuts?" he asked.

I exhaled, finally able to breathe and think. "I'm being driven there."

"What the hell's going on?" he demanded.

I moved to the corner of his single bed and sat. The familiar contours of the room materialized around me—his wooden dresser with its five drawers, the baseball trophies on top, the posters of two of his favorite baseball gods thumbtacked to the walls, the laptop humming on the nightstand next to his cell phone, both plugged in and charging. Beside them stood an empty beer can. I could smell it on the air, on him.

My gaze circled back to Steve. His magnificent body wore only a pair of old red briefs that, like all his clothes, seemed to love his anatomy. Not lost on me in my confusion was how tented those briefs were—morning wood or the result of my sudden appearance, I couldn't determine the cause of his excitement.

"I was sleepwalking," I said.

"What?"

"Into the woods. To that damned oak tree."

Steve folded his arms. "Dude, seriously?"

"For real. Look at me—look at what I'm wearing!"

He did.

"Can you take me home?"

Steve didn't comment at first, only stood there, arms folded and silent.

I got up and moved directly beside him. The stale smell of beer thickened. "Do you know all that I've done, everything I've risked, to be here with you again? I need your help now—why can't you see that?"

Steve unfolded his arms and judged me with a cutting look. "Dude, chill out. You show up here in your underwear acting and talking crazy, how do you think I'll react?"

He turned toward the dresser and opened the second drawer from the bottom. From it, he fished out two pairs of shorts.

"Here," Steve said.

I pulled them on. Steve dressed, adding the first T-shirt he retrieved from the middle drawer. Saying nothing, he sat on the bed and laced up his sneakers, not bothering with socks, and grabbed his keys off the top of the dresser. Wordless, we exited the house, followed the path of pavers around to the driveway, and got into his truck. He started the ignition. The sound at the early hour struck my ear like thunder, a clear indication of guilt, though no crime had been committed.

Steve put the truck in reverse and pulled onto Dean Avenue, threw it into drive, and continued on to Juniper Road. In front of my father's house, he decided to speak.

"I know you're not telling me everything, Oliver," he said.

"I'm telling you everything I can."

Steve shook his head. "I'm gonna be a cop. Do you think I won't know when a suspect's lying?"

"So now I'm a suspect and a liar?"

"You know more than you're telling me, so why don't you come clean?"

On this day, I was now expected to divulge the details of my trip through time to not one but two men, each the love of my life in different times—Before Bradley and After Steve.

"I will, Steve, I promise," I said, and that was the God's honest. "But I can't now. You'll really think I'm crazy."

Steve laughed, but the sound lacked all humor. "I'm already starting to think you are, buddy."

"Maybe I am. Only a crazy person would sacrifice all that I have to be here with you."

I moved to get out. He grabbed my wrist, holding me in place for another moment.

"Thanks for the rescue, Steve," I said. "I plan to return the favor. I mean it."

He released me. I fast-marched across the lawn and into the house. Mercifully, my father was in the shower. I sneaked into my room, slapped on deodorant, and dressed for work—the night over, the day begun with few knowing what had led up to its start.

I powered through work, throwing myself into the job in order to distract myself from what had happened. My argument with Steve nearly matched my horror over sleepwalking to the cursed oak in terms of the dark shadow it cast over my day.

"Canfield," Fenster called. "Go see Jonesy—he has a mission for you."

I ceased sweeping the floor. "What kind of mission?"

Fenster straightened as much as his potbelly allowed. "I'm sorry, do you have me confused with Jonesy?"

I saluted and pounded out through the rear exit to the stockyard. Jonesy and two of the other summer hires were loading rolled sod onto the back of one of our trucks for delivery.

"Good, you're here," Jonesy said.

"Been here all along," I said.

He gave me a look. "Lose the 'tude, okay?"

"No 'tude to lose—Fenster sent me out here."

Jonesy continued to dissect me through narrowed eyes. "I was hoping you'd be up to making your first delivery."

I'd made hundreds, but I kept that useless fact to myself. "Sure. Anything you need."

"What I need is this to get where it's going on time to a customer." He handed me the order slip. "That's the address. Think you're up for unloading it yourself? We're shorthanded and super busy today."

They weren't, and it wasn't. My muscles weren't the underdeveloped boiled noodles they'd been when I arrived. I glanced at the order slip and scanned the address—92 Lakewood Drive. "I'll manage."

I jumped in and drove away. Shorthanded? Lazy was more like it. Lakewood, at this time, was a new development of high-end construction with views of the harbor. The sod delivery looked about enough to cover the short span of what amounted to a front or backyard, given the paltry size of the lots between houses squeezed nearly on top of one another.

I drove with the windows open, pondering the night's travails and those that had followed at morning's start. Training my focus on Bradley didn't lessen my burden. I would be honest with him. About everything. I decided while seated behind the wheel to come completely clean. If there was anyone I could share the truth with, it was the man I'd one day wed.

That concession removed much of the weight off my chest and shoulders. It was like a switch got flipped, and I remembered that when Bradley and I worked through problems together in the past—or future—we'd always solved them. It was only when I tackled dragons on my own that I found myself spiraling counterclockwise through time.

It was a wise decision and a sound plan. I continued to 92 Lakeside. In record time, my first delivery was complete. I seemed back on track to take over Jonesy's job down the line as I had in the other reality. From there I'd own the Friday Harbor Garden Center, as I was always meant to.

Easy peasy.

I assumed so, anyway.

I walked outside and into the sunshine, exhausted from the day's demands but also elated, because Bradley was waiting, as I knew he would be. Broken clocks can be trusted to tell the correct time twice a day, but Bradley could always be depended upon. He'd never let me down, not even when I failed him.

Relief washed over me. I got into his car and saw the canvas shopping bag in the back seat. That tote would endure into our future, becoming one of a dozen we took with us to the store because we both hated plastic bags.

"Afternoon, sexy," he said.

I looked at him, at that charming smile, which he would wear more often than scowls or frowns. He was happy by nature and would continue to be—except when I killed that smile with my behavior over Steve Ranley's death.

"I love you," I said, and then I crushed my mouth over his.

The words were out, unable to be taken back. I wasn't worried about my confession. In that other time and place, I was the first of us to say "I love you." It had come on the heels of that fifth date, during highly anticipated sex with the handsome young lifeguard who'd romanced me out of my grief following Steve's death.

He drove toward the big lake, passing the Bella Vista villa. "That's where we're staying, my folks, me, and my sister."

"Kate," I said.

He eyed me from the edge of his sunglasses. "Yeah, that's right. How'd you know?"

I didn't say. Full disclosure was coming. Best to not reveal all while the car was still in motion.

He pulled onto a dirt road that ran down to the lake, one of the dozens of boat launches scattered around Friday Harbor. The early-evening sunlight dappled the water. Birds sang in the surrounding trees.

Bradley reached into the back seat for the tote.

"One of the things you'll find out about me is that I love a good, simple—"

"Picnic," I interjected.

Bradley settled back against his seat. He opened the top of the tote. Inside were two kinds of cheese, a cheese knife, and something I hadn't anticipated: a little green paper box filled with wild blackberries.

"That's right," he said, his tone suspicious.

"Blackberries?" I asked.

Bradley continued to study me. "Sure. You told me they were your favorite. I passed this little roadside stand—a card table run by kids who picked them in the woods."

They were the same kind I'd seen that very morning and had shared with Steve during our postcoital breakfast in the other timeline.

"And let me guess—Swiss cheese, your favorite."

"Okay, now you're really messing with my head," Bradley said.

"It gets better—or worse, depending on your outlook," I said. "Your favorite movie is *Buckaroo Banzai*. Your favorite book is *The Little Prince* by Antoine de Saint- Exupéry."

"You get all that off my FaceSpace page?"

I took a heavy swallow before answering. "No, FaceSpace won't tell me about the time your Aunt Loretta on your mother's side crashed the dirt bike. Or about the broken cookies."

All the color drained from his face. "How do you know about that?"

"About how in the second grade, you were handed cookies with the rest of the class, but all of yours were broken in the package? How upset you were? That it was, according to you, the last time you cried?"

Bradley sat, tense.

"I know all this and a hell of a lot more, my love, because, as I told you, you and I were meant to be together. And we will be. We're getting married, and we'll restore that little house. Oh, and it's absolutely vital that you also know I've traveled back in time from just over ten years into the future."

EX MARKS THE SPOT

Chapter 13

"Are you, like, *punking* me?"

Bradley exhaled a laugh that sounded desperate. I reached into the tote and scooped a handful of blackberries into my mouth. They were slightly tart and still warm from the sunlight their cells had absorbed. "Do I look like it?"

"No, which, I gotta say, is definitely freaking me out."

"Good."

"Good?"

"You should be freaked out. Trust me, I am too. But I also trust you more than any other person on the planet."

Bradley reached for the Swiss and the cheese knife. "Why's that?"

"Simple. Because time and time again, you've proven that you can be trusted. You're a great husband. Believe me, the stuff I complain about is so minor, it isn't worth mentioning. Closing the cap on the organic dish soap we use at Blackberry Corners so it doesn't dry up—that sort of thing."

He sliced off a chunk of Swiss. "Blackberry Corners?"

"Our home. That little house I showed you. You're gonna restore her completely. Every foot of that house will boast your capable touch. We're going to be very happy there. Well, mostly."

"Mostly?" he asked while chewing.

Here it comes, I thought.

I opened the crackers and dove in.

"Do you remember the day I told you about my friend?"

"Sure. The one you said you're trying to help."

"Technically, we're more than friends."

"You said you weren't a couple!"

"We're not. Friends with, you know, *bennies*. The truth is, I wasn't supposed to meet you for another two years. He's the guy I'm with in this time, the one I'm meant to be with."

A wounded look crossed Bradley's face. "And he's out of the picture when you and I cross paths in the future?"

"Completely out of it. Erased. On August 30, he crashed his truck into a tree right around the corner from where he lives. Something happened. I wound up back here in this time, before Steve's accident. At first I thought I was here to stop it, to save him. Now, I think, well . . . that I'm really here to save *us*, you and me. To remove the shadow of his death so we can be together without it hanging over us, haunting us."

He reached into my hand and took two crackers. "If we weren't supposed to meet for two years—"

"What are we doing here, together at this time? That might be my fault. I've done things out of order, changed the way it all went down the first time. Maybe I shouldn't have. But I had to see if it was possible to alter the outcome at the end of August. Time isn't rigid. I believe I've sent these ripples out into the world as a result. Cheese me."

Bradley handed me a wedge of Swiss as he munched, crunched.

"These ripples of yours could be rewriting the future," he said. "We weren't going to stop here on our way through New England. The plan was to continue through to Jersey, but one morning we pulled into a gas station in town and bumped into your dad. He saw our boat and told us about the marina, so we stayed."

I pondered his statement. That first morning when my father had dropped me off at the garden center—he'd bemoaned being low on gas! "That's what the Crazy Plant Lady said. A warning that the ripples would change things."

"Crazy—?"

"Plant Lady. Ms. Burch. She's the nutty Sophomore Biology teacher I had two years ago. She knows plants even better than I do. She's always at the garden center, even in the future, when I own the place."

I told him about our future work lives.

"Me, a cop?"

"I think you really only did it because of Steve Ranley, for me," I said. "But you look extremely hot in your uniform."

"Hells, yeah, I do. Or will. *Crackers.*"

I fed him two. As our insane conversation continued, it struck me how comfortable the discussion was, how easy it flowed. Not that I should have worried. That was how our relationship had always been. I was right to think that, together, he and I could solve any problem, even one as big as our present situation.

"So what do you want to do?" he asked.

I reached for the sweating bottle of seltzer still in the tote and handed Bradley the can of soda. We cracked open our drinks.

"On August 30 I plan to stop him from getting behind the wheel and driving into that rainstorm," I said. "After that, I dunno . . . does time reset? Do I go back to the future?"

"Great question, Marty McFly," he said.

I playfully smacked his bare knee.

"Ow," he complained.

"Baby," I fired back.

We were together, in our familiar successful roles.

Turning serious, Bradley asked, "What can I do to help?"

"You're doing it. You're here with me. Even after all the Sturm und Drang I've dumped onto your lap."

He smiled. The last of the sun dipped behind the trees. I reached up and removed his sunglasses. His eyes weren't gemstones, but they were more beautiful to me than sapphires. "If we are as close as you say, least I can do is try to help rescue this other dude's life so we can be a couple, not a threesome. Unless you like a—"

"No, you're all I need."

I kissed him. So close, the smell of his body, the sweetness from the blackberries and soda, and my own overwhelming gratitude to have him once more in my life all conspired to remove barriers.

"About that fifth date," I sighed.

"Screw the fifth date," he growled.

We shuffled food back into the tote. Bradley whipped the bag into the back seat and then tore off his T-shirt, baring his sculpted chest. I kissed him again before moving lower, lower.

On my way down, my inner critic taunted me. *There you go again, Oliver—messing around some more with the established track of time.*

We both climaxed twice. Part of an early moon rose over the lake along with plenty of stars. I rested my head on Bradley's bare shoulder. He wrapped his arm around me.

"I love you too," he said.

"You do?"

He scratched his bearded chin over the top of my head. I chuckled. "Do you doubt me?"

I looked up, his handsome face barely visible in the new night's darkness. "Hey, I've had a lot longer to get used to the idea."

He pondered my little joke. "I could be wrong, but I gotta admit— from the moment I saw you in the grocery store, I felt something."

"Lust," I teased.

"Well, yeah, that. But it was more. I wanted to meet you. Is that love at first sight or a kind of second sight? You tell me."

I toyed with a few strands of his chest hair, curling them with my finger. "I made up my mind that even though I was with Steve in this time the first go-around that after bumping into you, I only wanted to be with you. What he and I had for that short time wasn't really love. It took my being here with you—remembering the love we shared—to remove the scales from my eyes."

Bradley reached for his discarded shirt and pulled it on. We dressed awkwardly within the confines of his rental car.

"It's getting late. I should take you home," he said.

"Okay. Thanks, babe."

Bradley grinned. "For what?"

"For listening. For believing me. And for the best rapid speed dates four to five I could have wanted."

He grabbed my knee and squeezed it, started the car, and backed down the dirt road until we were on pavement and headed for my father's house.

Bradley parked along the street. The house sat dark. I needed a shower. I needed Bradley more.

"So what's next?" he asked.

"Sleep. Work. *You*," I said.

"I'll pick you up tomorrow night. We can continue our talk. And, you know, the other stuff."

I leaned over and kissed him. He held me in a way that was both new and familiar, a way I needed.

"I love you, Bradley," I said.

"Love you too, Oliver."

I got out. Bradley did the same.

"Thought I'd walk you to the door," he said without my asking why. "Figured it was only right, considering how much we love each other."

I grinned. "I'll let you."

I extended my hand. Bradley took it. We ambled up the driveway, our closeness hidden from view by the night. Or so I believed.

A figure moved out of the shadows near the garage. Steve Ranley stormed over to us, the anger on his face visible in the paltry glow of the nearest streetlamp.

"*Jesus*," Bradley gasped, startled.

Steve sized up Bradley before pulling me away from him, breaking our handhold. The smell of beer on his breath rained onto my face.

"So, this is what you've been doing behind my back?" Steve huffed.

"Wait a second," Bradley attempted.

Steve whirled and shoved Bradley back. The same level of horror that had greeted my day would end it. Bradley stood his ground. They were evenly matched in terms of height, muscle, and rage.

"It isn't what you think," I said.

"It isn't?" Steve spat.

Another moment passed, and I was sure punches would be thrown. In an effort to avoid that, I stepped between the two combatants—a serious mistake. Steve's right fist caught me in the cheek. Pain exploded up the side of my face, and then I was falling, falling.

"Oh, man, I'm so sorry," Steve apologized, standing over me with his face now mostly in shadow.

Bradley shoved Steve aside and took his place in my view of the night sky and stars. "Get the hell away from him, dude! In fact, why don't you scram before I pound you into the dirt?"

I laughed at the horrific irony of the statement and then winced. Bradley remained over me, concern written across the part of his face I could see. "What's so funny?"

"Scram? I half expected you to say '*am-scray.*' Now that would have been groovy."

Bradley shook his head and helped me to stand. I regained my footing. Steve stood several paces away, his back to us, hands on his hips.

"Steve, let me explain," I said.

"Don't bother," he fired back, walking away.

I watched him go down Juniper Road. Bradley moved closer.

"So, that's him?"

I nodded. "Steve."

"If it's any consolation, I don't think he meant to clock you."

I licked the raw inside of my cheek. "No, babe, that fuck-knuckle had you written all over it."

Bradley took me back into his arms.

"Sure you're okay? Need me to get you an ice pack or some aspirin?"

I patted his flank. I'd made my choice, and it was the right one, even at the cost of some blood. "I'll be fine. Just for the record, you've never hit me."

"Of course I haven't."

He kissed the top of my head. After a while, we resumed our walk to the front door. Bradley bid me goodnight. How desperately I wanted him to come inside and stay the night like all our future years at Blackberry Corners. At that instant, as he walked away, I ached as much for Bradley as I'd ever mourned Steve Ranley throughout the decade following his death in that other reality.

I made deliveries while Jonesy and his boys slacked off. I cleaned up around the place. I provided my wealth of knowledge to customers who were clueless about mulch or composting, lawn care and ornamentals. I took great pride in my job, but that confidence wasn't appreciated—not by Jonesy, who I clashed with more and more as the month of July progressed, and with Fenster who, twice, warned me about my attitude.

"What attitude? I know what I'm talking about," I said on that last day of July, not a full hour into my shift.

"My office—*now*," Fenster said.

I navigated behind him in the wake of the cloying aftershave he'd splashed on to cover up the fact he hadn't showered that morning. Over the course of the few years I worked for him, first as a laborer and then as the garden center's manager, Jim Fenster and I had butted heads on many occasions. I was always grateful to him, not only for the opportunity he gave me but also for the fair market price he settled on that allowed me to purchase the place.

Something in his tone was different.

I entered the office, a too-tight prison cell littered with folders, stacks of old receipts, and the details left over from decades of ownership. During my renovation, this part of the garden center would become floor space.

"I'm not happy," Fenster said.

"I got that from your twitching eyebrow," I said, hoping to diffuse his mood.

Fenster was not amused. "I've had several complaints about you, Canfield."

"Complaints?" I parroted. "From whom?"

"Jonesy, for one. He tells you to do something, you answer with attitude. My niece too. She says you interrupt her when she's speaking to customers because you know the plant business so much better than the rest of us. I've seen it for myself. It's like you think you're God's gift to the petunias."

I laughed. It was a stupid thing to do, especially given that Fenster hadn't meant it as a joke.

"You think this is funny?" he asked.

"No," I said. "But what is laughable is your niece—she's stealing from you. Not a lot, and she's been more careful to write hand receipts for cash customers, bypassing the register. You'll catch on in about a year. As for Jonesy, he's great at delegating work to others. As far as actually doing any himself, not so much. You'll wise up to that fact too, in due time. Hey, you ought to cut right to the chase and fire them both now and make me your new manager. You'll have some great years as a result before you retire and sell the place to me."

It was all out of my mouth before I could censor or stop it. Fenster looked at me like I was beyond crazy.

"Fire Jonesy?" he snorted. "Sell the nursery—to *you?* What kind of an idiot do you think I am? Hell, what kind of an idiot are you, Canfield?"

He reached into the mess on his desk and pulled out a white envelope, the kind our biweekly insults came in. My heart galloped. It couldn't be.

But it was.

Fenster handed me the envelope.

"We're coming up on the end of the season," he said, delivering a speech I'm sure he'd used plenty of summers.

"No, don't do this," I pleaded.

"And I'm afraid I have to let you go."

"What about autumn—mums and pumpkins? And the Christmas trees after that?"

EX MARKS THE SPOT

Fenster shook the envelope at the end of two clenched fingers. "Take it and get out."

I made a grab for the envelope, which contained a handwritten check for the last of my hours. I'd been fired from the job that, in the other timeline, had become my livelihood. *Fired*, months before I'd begun that job in the first reality.

Not believing what had happened, I walked out through the main entrance, where all my betrayers had gathered to watch me leave.

"*Ripples*," I whispered, plodding into the early-morning heat.

Chapter 14

Sprawled on my spine, I stared at the ceiling, paralyzed from shock. What had happened wasn't meant to—I'd never received so much as a warning from Jim Fenster. While reviewing the events leading up to my dismissal, I saw my mistakes. I'd approached the job through eyes aware of the future, not with the attitude of the past, which I should have. And I'd bypassed the grocery store, gone right to the garden center months ahead of schedule. I doubted there was any way to make things right again after what I'd said on my way out. If there was, I couldn't see it.

The walk home had been the longest yet. Every cell in my body ached. My head pounded. This couldn't be! Only any time I needed proof that it had, indeed, happened, all I had to do was shoot a look over at my desk to see the white envelope containing my final paycheck.

With his niece and Jonesy, Fenster was screwed. But in revealing knowledge brought back from the future, I'd screwed myself worse. What else had I erased through the concentric ripples I'd created in making seemingly small changes to the timeline?

At least I still had Bradley. *Bradley*—he was due to pick me up after work. I reached for my cell and dialed his number. He answered on the second ring.

"Hey, bruiser," he said lightly. "How's your cheek?"

"Bruised," I said. "But not nearly as much as my ego. Something happened."

"What?" he asked.

I sat up and gave him the short answer.

"You all right, Oliver?"

"No, Bradley. In the future I told you about . . . that place is a major reason we have the life we've created."

I heard him exhale. "I'm sure it can be salvaged."

Ever the optimist, I thought.

"So don't pick me up there. I'll be here at my father's house."

"Groovy," he said.

I closed my eyes, imagined him at the beach, so handsome and always so happy. What I wanted was for him to whisk us both ten years forward through time, back to our little house and our lives there. But that couldn't be, because our life together at Blackberry Corners would still suffer beneath the pall of Steve's death.

"See you later," I said. "Love you."

"Love you too, babe," he whispered. He must have been within earshot of family, I guessed.

Apart from lacking the apparatus to return to our future time and place, I hadn't yet completed my mission.

Tomorrow was the first day of August.

I looked at the clock on my phone. Hours yet to go before Bradley was due. I jumped up and was walking again.

An hour later, I'd cashed my last paycheck from the garden center. Half of it would go to my father. I'd hold onto the rest, parceling it out as needed. With my heart feeling like it had lodged in my throat, I trudged over to Victory Supermarket. There, I filled out a job application. On the long way around town and back in the direction of Old Coach Road, I spied a sign and again altered my course. My legs would be as magnificent as Steve Ranley's by the end of this summer.

On approach to the high school, I thought of Steve, of his rage. It wasn't that I thought he was jealous of Bradley so much as hacked off that Bradley had denied him the easy and reliable option of relief I offered. It was more about competition than emotion. I now realized Steve didn't love me, and that he never had in the true sense of love. My own understanding had evolved enough for me to see that what I felt for him had only been lust mixed with a juvenile's crush. It didn't hold up against what I had with Bradley.

Friday Harbor High appeared before me, the long brick prison I'd been released from but was willingly returning to like an inmate unable to function on the outside. Several cars lined the faculty driveway, a few dozen more in student parking. Summer school was in session.

I made my way through the library doors, cut left, and entered the science wing. I hadn't been to this part of my past in ten years, according to my secret memory taken back from the future, but I found my way to an empty classroom easy to identify thanks to its see-through man and authentic human skeleton, wired and hanging on display like the most gruesome Halloween decoration possible. Part of me recalled how, in tenth grade, Ms. Burch had remarked that the skeleton had come from Asia, where many such oddities to grace American classrooms originated.

The door stood open. No students sat at desks. I knocked. No one answered.

I cut through the room to a door at the far end. Beyond was the greenhouse where the Crazy Plant Lady—not quite as crazy in this time period—grew vegetables, Venus flytraps, and, as rumors went, high-grade pot.

An off-key song in a woman's voice greeted me a few steps shy of reaching the greenhouse door. Ms. Burch was bent over the cultivations, singing to the denizens of the small operation. I identified eggplant and tomatoes, a few fanged horrors with an appetite for insects, but no marijuana plants. So much for that particular legend.

But it was legends that I was here to discuss.

Clearing my throat, I announced myself. Ms. Burch came out of her trance and jolted up.

"Oh, you scared me," she said, straightening.

"I didn't mean to. I'm sorry."

She recovered and narrowed her eyes. "You're the boy from the garden center. What are you doing here?"

"Hoping to continue our discussion. Remember, we had a chat a few weeks ago about time travel?"

She brightened. "Yes, through the rings of trees. I do remember."

I scanned the greenhouse. "You've done a remarkable job here. Your wards all look well cared for and healthy."

She smiled. "I like to sing to them." And then she folded her arms, assuming a defensive posture. "If you're here about buying weed—"

"No, I swear. Just time travel."

"Time travel," she sighed. "I've wrapped my mind around the concept, and I have to say I'm agreeable to the possibility. The mysteries of the plant kingdom are such that just about anything is possible. Consider cycads, if you will—holdovers from as far back as the Jurassic period when they covered the planet. We're talking more than two hundred million years ago—*201.3*, in fact!"

I nodded. "I know. And I'm convinced time travel of a kind is possible. What I also wanted to ask you is less about science, more about mythology."

"Mythology?"

"Legends. Lore. Things supernatural that are associated with trees. Evils that could disguise themselves as cycads. Or oaks."

She drew in a deep breath and released it. "The first that come to mind are dryads—nymphs or spirits that inhabit trees from Greek mythology. In fact, the word 'drys' in Greek refers specifically to oak trees. Then you have Norse mythology and Yggdrasil, the giant tree that connects different realms and worlds. In Madagascar you have the man-eating tree, a tentacled horror believed to feed on . . . you guessed it. And in Nicaragua, natives spoke of the vampire vine, which caught hold of the unsuspecting and drank the blood of its ensnared human victims. Then, of course, you have your garden-variety trees that have been cursed by circumstance— *garden-variety*, get it?"

I realized I'd listened with my eyes wide and not blinking, my mouth hanging open.

"But they're only legends," Ms. Burch said.

I thought about reminding her that most legends have their basis in fact but remembered that she was crazy enough already and would grow more so in the years to follow. I forced a smile and thanked her.

"This tree," she asked, "the one capable of great evil. Is it also the source of time displacement?"

I nodded, turned, and marched out of the greenhouse.

"Then be careful," she called after me. "It won't be denied that which it craves most!"

I was showered and dressed when Bradley drove up to the front of the house. It was earlier than my usual nights of late, and my father hadn't yet walled himself behind the door to his bedroom.

"Who's that—Warren Rudd?" he asked.

"No, Bradley MacIntyre."

My father unscrewed the cap of his beer. "What's he doing here?"

"We're friends," I said, feeling my face flush as the conversation turned intrusive.

"Yeah? Like you and the Ranley boy?" my father asked, a cutting note in his tone.

I faced him.

"He hasn't been around in a while, but for weeks he was always here. You think I didn't know—or that the two of you got into my beer?"

My pulse quickened. It had been quite a long time since I was put on the defensive over my right to privacy or my sexual identity, but I remembered the mistakes I'd already made, big ones, over the misuse of knowledge regarding the future. I decided to play it safe.

"It's not what you think," I said.

My father grumbled, "What I think? I think my son has never dated a girl, sneaks around after dark with Steve Ranley, and thinks I'm clueless."

I readied to fire off a comeback.

"But I also think Bradley MacIntyre is a much better choice, so I'll give you credit."

"Thanks," I said on my way out the door.

Even now, years earlier, my father loved Bradley like a favorite son. Relief washed over me. I could live with that.

We returned to the lake and sat for a while without speaking. Clouds swept in. The smell of rain hung in the air.

"You know," Bradley said, breaking the silence, "I love the future you described. But if it isn't cast in granite, that doesn't mean it's the only one."

In addition to his optimism, Bradley could also be counted on to point out the obvious—even when I didn't want to hear it.

"What?"

"Okay, so say you don't buy the garden center and we don't get the house."

"Those are some ugly 'ifs,'" I said.

"But that doesn't mean we don't prevail, that we won't succeed," he continued. "Maybe the setting's different, but the main cast of characters remains the same."

I didn't want to hear it, despite the hope his explanation provided. "No garden center or Blackberry Corners?"

"Hear me out," Bradley said. "The hardware store my family owns in Neptune City—we sell plants in the spring and autumn. Not like the garden center, but enough that it wouldn't hurt to have someone around who actually knows something about them. Hell, I don't—couldn't tell a begonia from a turnip."

I laughed. "One's a flower, the other's a root vegetable."

"See? You'd be perfect there. And we even sell Christmas trees every year on the lot starting the Saturday after Thanksgiving."

"What about the rest of it? The rest of our lives?"

Bradley pressed his spine flat against the driver's seat in an attempt to stretch out his long legs and sighed. "I'm sure I'll look hella hot in that police uniform."

"Trust me, babe—you do."

"But it seems to me I only went that route to satisfy you. Now, imagine, if you will . . . *me* in a ratty pair of blue jeans, an old flannel shirt so threadbare you can practically see through parts of it, old work boots, and a blue apron while I'm mixing paint and helping customers buy the right screws for the job."

"Sexy," I agreed.

"I know, right? Who needs a police uniform when all of this . . . " He aimed a thumb at himself. ". . . smells like woodchips and turpentine?"

"When you put it like that, I'm convinced," I said, taking his hand. "Especially knowing you can provide the right screws for the job."

Bradley raised my hand to his mouth and kissed it. Our eyes met in the falling shadows, and what passed between us needed no words. Whatever shape our future took, it would be happy and fulfilling, so long as we were together.

"We'll have cats," he said.

"I like cats."

"Two, one for each lap. They'll live with us in the apartment upstairs, over the store."

"There's an apartment over the hardware store?"

"Of course, more than one actually. I'm in the small unit, corner of the building. Great views."

"Of what?"

"The parking lot mostly." He eyed me. "Don't you know all of this from the future?"

I gripped his hand. "By that point, your folks had sold the place and moved to Florida."

My words threatened his happiness. "Oh."

Bradley released me and went fishing through the catchall between our seats. He pulled out a business card and handed it to me.

"Here. In case that changes."

I took the card. *Neptune City Hardware*, it read. A picture of a paint can and brush decorated it, along with the address and phone number.

"This is better than an engagement ring," I said.

Bradley's smile returned. "Consider it proof that, no matter what, we'll be together after the 30th of August, whether in Friday Harbor restoring Blackberry Corners of someplace else, like Neptune City, selling monkey wrenches."

I clutched the card. "I'll sleep with it under my pillow, I promise."

"You'd better."

We kissed. And then we kissed some more. All my worries—Steve, the garden center, coming out to my father, and demons lurking in cursed oak trees—vanished. I was with Bradley, and in all of time and space, it seemed like all that mattered.

"Laid off?" my father said.

"That's what happened. Laid off. Let go. Last one in, first one cut during the end-of-season trim," I said. "But don't worry—I'm already applying for jobs to replace it."

He held the envelope containing room and board for August and extended it back in my direction. "Here, take it."

"No. While I'm still living here, I intend to pay my own way."

"I respect that. And I have to tell you, it's about time you cut that damn mop of yours."

"Don't worry—I'll never let it grow that long again."

He nodded, pocketed the money, and left for the marina. I was relieved to see him go. My first coming out in that other timeline following Steve's death hadn't gone nearly as smoothly, but I was still a mess of raw nerves around my father when it came to the subject of my true identity. That wouldn't alter much for at least the next ten years if it jibed with the other reality, though it was no longer to be trusted, considering how much had already changed as a result of my corrupting the course of time.

I'd told Bradley how much my father liked him, both in the future and in this new version of the past.

"I want you to meet my family," he said. "Why don't you join us tonight for dinner?"

I liked my in-laws, the MacIntyres. In that other time, we were always cordial, even though I knew they resented that Bradley had moved to Friday Harbor to be with me instead of following them south. Maybe that too would change in the days and years to follow.

My cell rang. I picked it up without checking the caller's identification.

"Hello?"

"Yes, I'm trying to reach Oliver Canfield."

"Speaking."

"This is Dave O'Neill from Victory Supermarket. How are you today?"

Two days later, I was standing at the end of the checkout counter's conveyor belt, putting cans into the bottoms of plastic bags, delicate groceries on top.

Chapter 15

Fog drifted over the morning, a dense soup in no hurry to disperse even after the sun rose.

I walked along the side of the road, headed to the job I hated, wondering if I'd walked out of one world and into another—a realm of man-eating trees, vampire vines, and dryads. A bird cried out sharply from somewhere in that miasma. I looked down, the edge of the pavement my only guide.

The sound of a vehicle coming up behind me sent me farther onto the shoulder. The fog thinned as it passed—a truck. And not just any pickup. Steve's familiar ride with the black paint and gold racing stripe braked on the road. My heart galloped. He put the truck into a slow reverse and met me in the middle.

The passenger's side window lowered. "Need a lift?" Steve asked.

I got in, not so much for the ride but to say what needed saying. August was fading. That ominous day marked in history in violent strokes of red would soon arrive.

He sat behind the wheel dressed in a white T-shirt, jeans, and new sneakers—I knew before seeing that flash of bare ankle that he wasn't wearing socks.

"Steve," I said.

He hesitated from driving away. I wondered if we had somehow drifted out of time's normal flow and into the fog, the only two people together in some kind of pocket universe. But the appearance of another car in the opposite lane dispelled that theory. Steve gave the truck some gas.

"The garden center?" he asked.

I shook my head. "No, supermarket."

He eyed me from the periphery. "Victory?"

The words tasted sour as I spoke them. "I got laid off from the garden center."

"Oh."

He drove on. The fog thinned more. The outside world surfaced from the grayness, though not completely.

"I left her for you," he said. "I broke up with my girlfriend to be with you."

I shook my head. "No, Steve. You did all that for *you*—and that's okay, really."

He pulled over to the side of the road but refused to look at me. "What we did . . ." he sighed.

"Was great," I said. "Unforgettable. I have no regrets, and neither should you. I only wish it hadn't ended the way it did."

He forced his gaze over. "Sorry about that punch."

"It happened. I'm tough—a lot more than people think."

Steve's focus lingered. "That other dude."

"Bradley."

"Do you, you know—"

"Love him? Yes."

Steve sucked down a heavy breath and settled back against the seat, his eyes now aimed at the driver's side window. "So all that stuff you said about loving me was bullshit?"

"No, it was the truth."

He stayed turned away from me until I set my hand on his upper arm.

"*Steve*," I said. "You have no idea how much I loved you. More than a human being should be capable. But there's so much about that love you don't know."

Steve turned back in my direction, his expression stony. "Tell me."

"What you said to me, more than once, was that I was different. That you sensed I knew more than I was telling you. That's all true too. I am different. This might be difficult to believe, but I'm really from ten years into the future. I came back in time. Bradley—in the future we're married. There was an accident. There will be another one on August 30 if I don't stop it from happening. You died in that accident, Steve. Crashed your truck into that big, ugly oak tree on South Main. For the next decade, your ghost haunts my days and nights. I think that's the reason I came back in time—to stop the accident and save you."

While I regurgitated my insane tale, Steve listened, not interrupting. For the next several seconds after, he maintained the same stiff, unblinking pose.

"Say something, please," I pleaded.

Steve broke focus with me, put the truck into drive, and motored forward.

"Steve?"

He shook his head. "If you didn't want to be with me, all you had to do was say so, not try to sell me some fucked-up load of bullshit."

"It's not—"

"*Enough*, Oliver," he barked. "In spite of what you think, I do care about you. I did."

We drove on. He didn't speak another word to me after that. I got out of his truck and turned away, facing the grocery store, my version of Hell in the flesh.

No comets appeared in the sky. Fireworks didn't go off, their cannonade announcing the hour. In the darkness of my room, however, I sensed the approach of midnight on a cellular level, a cosmic one. Reaching for my phone, I checked the time—11:59. As I stared, not daring to blink, the numbers advanced. Time asserted its pull. Midnight had arrived.

We had crossed over into the 30th of August, the same day in that other reality in which Steve Ranley died and time unraveled.

My next breath came with difficulty. Breathing for a while stopped being easy or even involuntary. I sucked down a hit of air, convinced I'd pass out at any second. I sat up, slipped beside the window, and inhaled. The air had attained a dry, cool note following several New England dog days—that slight chill indicating that summer was surrendering to autumn and soon to be over.

In the other timeline, August 31 and every day after had existed beneath the shadow of Steve's death. Nothing I'd done in this do-over had moved me any closer to understanding the events that had led me here—or any closer to stopping them. I'd lost the garden center—maybe the entire future that sprang forth as a result. After confessing he had felt more for me than only basic lust, Steve was done with me.

But I couldn't be done with him. Not yet. August 31 would be a whole new life, whether I succeeded in rescuing him or not.

My gaze wandered out into the shadows, past my neglected garden, toward the breaks in houses and the narrow vista looking onto Dean Avenue. I spotted the Ranley place, and my heart sank.

My phone buzzed, indicating a text had come in.

<u>You awake?</u> Bradley asked.

I dialed his number. "Yes."

"I figured as much. Any idea about tomorrow? I mean *today*."

"I don't know."

"I've cleared the entire day. I'm here if you need me. Whatever you need me for."

"Thanks, I appreciate that."

Closing my eyes, I rested my head on the windowsill. A cool breeze stirred the scarlet curtains.

"Babe?" he asked.

"Here, but I'm ready to go home."

"If today really is some kind of reset button, we could both be home by 7:17."

He said it in that usually upbeat Bradley MacIntyre way I loved so much but was unable to appreciate, given the weight of gravity and the dread blooming inside me like a cancer.

7:17.

It felt farther away than a decade. More like an eternity, in fact.

"I have to go alone," I said.

Bradley, who'd mother-henned me for most of that bright, late-August day, shook his head. "No; what if you need backup?"

"You're not a cop yet," I reminded him.

Throughout the afternoon, I'd caught myself growing less patient, more on edge. Bradley's sunny nature had surrendered to partial clouds as well, and I could see the frustration on his features.

"I'm sorry," I attempted.

Bradley nodded. "I know. But does he understand what he's putting you through—what he'll put *us* through for the next ten years if he doesn't listen?"

I couldn't answer that any more than I could sit still. My own skin seemed determined to constrict and crush me.

7:00.

"It's almost time," I said, the words escaping my mouth on a slight scream.

Bradley reached for me. I hugged him in a death grip. At 7:05 I exited the house.

Overhead, clouds now occluded the clear skies, and the humidity was back. I walked down Juniper Road in a daze, not sure of what I would say or do except that I'd stop Steve from getting behind the wheel of his truck and taking that doomed voyage down South Main Street. Houses passed by in a blur at the periphery. Eyes aimed straight ahead, I stared at the Ranley's place and the black pickup still parked in the drive.

Still there meant he was still alive. I would save him. I would undo ten years of heartbreak.

On the last hundred steps, emotion overwhelmed me, all of it for Steve. I remembered the sunny tartness of the blackberries on a morning from another time and reality that no longer existed. I could smell the clean scent of his sweat. I recalled every detail of his body, and what it was like to rest in his arms feeling safe, feeling special. He cared for me? I'm not sure why that should have been so surprising—he must have, the Steve from that other time and place and this one. For a decade after his death, I'd mourned him. But I'd also loved him. What did it matter if that love was mostly one-sided? It was real enough to me, and that made it real in the scheme of the universe.

My teeth chattered. Caustic, dry tears stung at the corners of my eyes. Ten more steps and I was even with and staring up at the front door. The door opened.

"Get back in here," Steve's father, Lloyd Ranley, shouted.

"Fuck you," Steve fired back.

Neither of the combatants had yet noticed me. I was witnessing the argument that had sent Steve to his death. A version of it, anyway.

The front door slammed shut. Steve continued down the steps, taking them two at a time, and then he hurried over to his truck, where he noticed me. The red rage on his face deepened.

"What are you doing here?"

"Rescuing you," I said.

I moved to his side. Steve shoved me away. As the tears spilled down my cheeks, I caught the smell of alcohol on him. That hadn't factored into the first timeline—there'd been no mention of it in his blood in any of the reports that followed the crash. But here it was again, so obvious that it triggered a memory of sharp clarity. The drinking—it was over me. If he got behind the wheel, I'd be the cause of his death more than that bloodthirsty tree.

If alcohol was the cause of the fight here, now, what had triggered the argument in that other time? Steve glared at me and my mind wandered, wondered. Was I also the reason? Had Steve cared for me more than I'd ever given him credit? Had he told his father about his secret, about *us*?

The cause didn't matter, only the effect. I hugged him again and didn't let go. Steve struggled.

"No," he spat, and then he sobbed the same response.

I held on, surprised at the level of muscle I'd built over the past two months. He ceased fighting and hugged me in return. We stood together, two lost souls. Thunder boomed. The sky opened up and rain fell—a warm, sticky downpour that matched my tears and reminded me of the deluge of blood from a summer night ten years ahead of this one.

So close together, our faces cheek to cheek, I told him I loved him. I *did* love him.

"Part of me always will," I promised, even as I lifted the keys out of his front pocket.

Thunder roared again. I looked into Steve's magnificent sapphire eyes. He cupped the side of my face and kissed me, full on the lips. The rain fell. I was so overwhelmed by that moment, so sure I'd saved him, that I'd failed to see the car driving closer from the direction of Juniper Road.

I can only imagine what the driver must have thought. Steve Ranley and I were in a passionate embrace, arms around one another, mouths locked.

Steve looked up. I heard the slosh of the tires through the puddles. Turning, I saw Bradley's rental on the road, idling. I released Steve and moved toward the front passenger's door. My fingers brushed the knob. I caught the wounded look on Bradley's face an instant before he gunned the gas and drove away.

"No, wait!" I called.

Bradley accelerated, taking that last stretch of Dean Avenue linking up to South Main Street. I reached into my pocket for my phone, intending to call him and explain—what had happened was an ending, no more. One last moment from the past that wouldn't carry into the future. I never made the call.

The clock on my phone screen read 7:16.

And as I watched, the minute hand advanced by one.

I dropped Steve's keys and ran in pursuit of Bradley. A few steps into it, the downpour intensified to deafening, and I lost sight of the way ahead. But, looking up, I saw the top of the cursed oak tree, and I knew that its thirst for the blood of those I loved would not be denied.

Instead of Steve, it would claim Bradley.

"*No,*" I wailed. "*Please, no!*"

I heard the impact, the unmistakable crunch of metal against trunk, followed by something powerful that my imagination translated into a thunderous cracking of bone. All around me, that cracking sound roared. Everything else waned, smothered by its intensity—the rain, Steve's shouts, my sobs.

It was time rippling, reshuffling.

Resetting.

The world around me went dark.

A million images flashed through my consciousness. The snapping of bones shorted out, replaced by a whine in my ear. I opened my mouth, but the one word I longed to utter reused to form. I licked my lips, opened my eyes. My vision stabilized.

I located my voice. *"Bradley?"*

From my left, blue police lights activated, their intensity sharp on the eye. In quick order, I looked around. I was in a car. I'd gone off the road—crashed headlong into that murderous oak! All of it came back to me—me in my hybrid, racing to get home to my husband on the ten-year anniversary of Steve Ranley's death.

Steve.

I'd gone back in time, returned to the past in order to save him from dying. And I had—I'd stopped him from crashing his truck into the cursed oak. Only . . .

Bradley had taken his place.

A dream, surely. But hadn't I asked myself the same question when I woke at the start of a lost summer a full decade behind me?

I looked around the car. Nothing matched the hybrid I drove. The car I was buckled into appeared to be an older model nowhere near as pristine as Bradley insisted it be kept.

The oak—before traveling counterclockwise, I'd run my car into it. I remembered the explosion as I struck. I glanced through the intact windshield. Deep, rainy woods loomed beyond the car, but the sinister colossus wasn't there. I peered lower. Set in front of the unfamiliar car was a massive tree stump, gray in the overcast light.

The oak was gone. For some while, judging by the condition of the stump.

A glance into the rearview added to the mystery. I didn't look eighteen but twenty-eight going on much older. My hair was a shaggy mop again.

A figure in a police uniform moved through the splinters of blinding electric blue, a man in uniform. I powered down the window.

"*Bradley?*" I called, hope burning briefly in my chest.

But it wasn't Bradley.

It was Officer Steve Ranley.

Chapter 16

Humidity swept into the strange car along with a host of green smells, a hint of Steve's sweat, and a bitter edge of what I knew was old alcohol leaching up through his pores.

"Oliver," he said, his voice a manly growl.

"You're alive," I gasped.

In the next second I recorded his handsomeness, grown hard around the edges—perhaps the last time in his life he'd be attractive—the heaviness in those tarnished sapphire eyes, and the gold wedding band on his ring finger when he set his hand at the base of the open window.

"What happened here?" he asked.

I glanced away, out the windshield. The oak tree was still gone, and had been for a long time. "The rain. I skidded off the road."

"You okay?"

I wasn't, but I nodded. Silence settled between us, one broken only by the heavy plunking of raindrops.

"Steve?" I eventually managed.

"Yeah, Oliver?"

"How's Officer MacIntyre?"

"MacIntyre?" Steve parroted.

"One of Friday Harbor's finest. Officer Bradley MacIntyre. You must know him."

Steve's eyes narrowed on me. "You sure you're all right?"

My lower lip ticked. Bradley—the sound of his rental car impacting against the bloodthirsty oak echoed through my thoughts.

"Oliver?"

"Yeah, I'm fine. Just want to go home. I really need to be home."

I took the wheel, gave the car some gas, and hit my right blinker, indicating my course south, toward Blackberry Corners.

"Home's that way," Steve said, pointing left.

Left, toward Juniper Road.

I drove right into the cathedral of trees and continued through the new, gray night. Tears welled in my eyes. I'd saved Steve, but in doing so had doomed Bradley, I was certain.

I exited the woods, drove on, and passed what had been the Friday Harbor Garden Center when I'd gotten behind the wheel of my hybrid in the final moments of the other timeline. To my shock, the nursery was gone, all the work I'd done erased. Instead of cultivated gardens welcoming customers to think green, the lot had been paved over. In place of the garden center was a used car dealership.

With my heart thudding, I turned onto Harbor Road and followed it to the house we had built together. In the gray gloom, I saw that nothing was as I'd known it. Blackberry Corners was gone, replaced by a McMansion-size modern construction.

The little bungalow had been raised instead of restored. Gone were all the gardens, the ornamental plantings, the fruit orchards. The blackberry patch never was.

The name on the mailbox read "Rudd."

Frozen, I sat behind the wheel outside Victory Supermarket. According to the nametag I found in the car's catchall, I was one of the store's assistant managers.

I reached into my back pocket for my wallet. My driver's license listed 19 Juniper Road as my residence. Everything I'd known in the other reality was gone, sacrificed for Steve Ranley, casualties of the ripples I'd created by tampering with the past. Those small, seemingly insignificant changes had widened, consuming my world.

I drove back to Juniper Road. The house looked as humorless and unwelcoming as always. The light was on above the kitchen sink. Not wanting to go inside, I sat in my car, aware of the lingering dregs of the rainstorm. After an hour, I got out and plodded across the overgrown lawn to the front door.

Inside, the house was a snapshot frozen in time, not much different than it had been ten years earlier. I switched on a light and viewed my surroundings as though for the first time, not the millionth.

On the refrigerator I found two schedules—one for my father's hours at the marina, one for mine at Victory. He hadn't retired, and all I could see in the numbers beneath my name was wasted time.

The sound of a door opening roused me from my gloom. My father wandered out of his room, looking older than he should have. We didn't make direct eye contact. Some things never changed, regardless of time.

"You're home," he said.

"Long day," I said.

"There's leftover pizza in the fridge."

"Thanks."

He nodded and turned back in the direction of his bedroom. "Good night."

"Night. Dad?"

He halted but didn't face me. "Yeah?"

"Do you know how Bradley is?"

"Bradley? You mean the MacIntyre boy?"

I choked down a dry swallow, sure the tears would resume. "Yeah, him."

"I don't know. Why?"

"I really need to know."

My father exhaled. "I haven't seen the MacIntyres since before the accident."

"The one on South Main Street?"

"They went back to New Jersey after that. Never came back the following summer, or any of the summers since. Can't really tell you how Bradley is because I don't know."

"Thanks."

"Why'd you want to know about him? That was a long time ago."

"Not to me it isn't," I said, switching off the light.

My bedroom was pretty much the same—old bed, dresser, desk, and new TV. Conspicuously absent from the setting were my grandfather's two bronze horses, which had occupied a place of honor at Blackberry Corners. I'd always thought of the pair as symbolic, a couple meant to be together.

I located my old senior high school yearbook on one of the shelves under the bed and flipped to the back and Steve's graduation picture. The page was crisp and showed no signs of constant visitation.

No secret tributes hid inside to mark the spot. When I looked at that photograph, I felt none of the fire or sadness that had resulted from previous viewings. I'd rescued Steve, simple as that. And following my sacrifice, he'd moved on. He was married, drinking, a cop. I was a weak version of the man I'd been in another reality, and I'd lost Bradley.

I closed the book and thought about returning it to the same shelf but didn't. The next morning, I dumped it in the trash.

I heard my father moving around and getting ready for work. It was August 31 according to the calendar and older, arcane methods of telling time. The big reset had happened, as prophesized. But while some casualties had been spared and resurrected, others paid the price for my hubris in corrupting the established flow of time.

I stared into the bathroom mirror. My hair was a mop and looked unattractive to me, my reflection that of a stranger. This version of me was. Without Bradley, I'd let my hair go wild, back to the way it was when I was eighteen.

Removing my T-shirt, I discovered an even more glaring change. The tattoo covered the patch of chest muscle over my heart. A scream powered from my stomach, clawed its way up my throat, and tore past my lips, unable to be trapped. The shriek echoed through my father's empty house, reminding me of my aloneness.

In shades of green, the tattoo was of a tree.

An oak tree, big and malevolent and sinister, a tree from a nightmare, permanently etched into my flesh.

I exited the house, dressed in navy work pants, a white button-down, a tie seemingly determined to choke me to death, and the apron with my nametag pinned to the upper right chest. Another in a long line of meaningless shifts at Victory Supermarket waited.

On my way down the walkway, I spotted the juniper tree Bradley had purchased on that long ago summer day at the garden center. Ten years had passed. Though overgrown like everything else on the property, the tree looked beyond healthy, thriving.

Earlier that morning, I'd peered through the threadbare scarlet curtains at the backyard to see the garden gone, only a few brambles among the weedy lawn to mark that it had ever been. Clearly, I hadn't kept up with mowing any more than I had sowing. But the juniper tree prospered. Standing there for a solid minute, it struck me why.

It was given and planted with love, my inner voice reminded.

The murderous oak tree was gone, but the juniper wasn't. My mind wandered—had one prevailed over the other? That remaining prescience from the lost reality reminded me of another bit of useless knowledge—of how an angelic presence in a juniper tree had shielded the prophet Elijah from pursuit by Queen Jezebel in the Old Testament.

Aware that I had smiled for the first time since my return to the future, I continued to my secondhand car for another day of living my secondhand life.

Long hours with few rewards, I discovered I'd accumulated a modest bank balance over the last decade. Nothing like what I'd saved as owner of the garden center, part of a two-income household with Bradley and living at Blackberry Corners. Still, enough to call upon on a rainy day.

September passed into October. Leaves changed color. It got colder, and I descended into a deep depression I couldn't climb out of.

A frigid, gray afternoon brooded outside the window. I paced the contours of my room, pulling at my long hair, hating it, hating myself more. What had started as an emptiness the size of an atom at the center of my chest gradually expanded to a black hole. Its hunger consumed me, and what little of my sanity remained was about to disappear.

With light, hope, energy, and flesh tumbling into the singularity's maw, so too had gone knowledge. The details I'd returned with from that other reality—my old life, which no longer existed— had grown blurry, like a barely remembered dream. Upon waking, holding onto it was like trying to embrace air, smoke—or a ghost.

I opened the bedroom closet. Inside were old clothes I hadn't worn in years, a pair of kicks that had been new ten years ago in that summer, and several cardboard boxes. I pulled the boxes out and tore them open. Most contained nothings—the castoffs of a life that didn't matter.

One box was labeled in marker—"For the Future." I pulled off the lid. Inside, wrapped in the scarlet scraps of the same material I'd used for the bedroom curtains, were my grandfather's bronze horses.

I unwrapped them and set them on my desk. There was nothing else in the box, or so I thought at first. While shuffling the fabric scraps aside, I found one other thing.

The hardware store's business card that Bradley had given me during our date on that long-ago summer night.

Hand shaking, I eyed the number.

An hour passed. I dialed. A woman picked up on the third ring.

"Neptune City Hardware, Kate speaking."

I tried to talk. My voice evaporated.

"Hello?" she said.

I cleared my throat. "Yes, is Bradley available?"

"Bradley?"

The next second passed with the slowness of eternity.

"Sorry, not today. Can I help you with something?"

"I really need to speak with Bradley."

"He's in on Saturday. Can I take a message?"

I ended the call, aware that my heart was in a mad gallop. It was, perhaps, beating—really beating—for the first time in more than a decade, despite evidence to the contrary.

I made the appointment with a mechanic for a tune-up, oil change, and general maintenance visit.

"Jersey?" he said. "No, I wouldn't travel all the way to the Garden State in this old heap. Might be a short trip. Or one way. You might not make it back."

"I'll take my chances," I said. "Besides, I've gone farther on more dangerous voyages and returned to tell the tale."

I took a few days off from work, left a note for my father, and set out early on Saturday morning. Even before I left Friday Harbor, it was snowing.

I drove, eyes aimed ahead on the road, not knowing what I would say other than tell him I loved him.

Early that afternoon, exhausted and bedraggled from my long journey south, I pulled into the parking lot of Neptune City Hardware. It was a charming place, with the store occupying the ground floor and apartment space above, just like he'd described. The lot was decorated with Christmas lights and fresh trees for sale.

I tipped a look into the rearview. Before leaving Friday Harbor, I'd gotten my hair cut. The face staring back, while aged beyond its twenty-eight years, at least now looked familiar.

I stepped out into the cold. The sweetness of balsam fir trees embraced me.

"Are you here about a tree?" a man asked.

At first, I couldn't turn. Facing him took every bit of energy I had. When I did, Bradley stood before me, a vision in old jeans, navy hoodie, work boots, and winter coat.

"You could say that," I answered, my voice barely louder than a whisper. "About a tree, sure."

Recognition crossed his handsome face. His beard was as perfect as I recalled.

"A juniper tree," I said. "*Juniperus* in Latin."

"Oliver?"

"You remember," I said.

He remained tense, stunned, even as I noticed his gaze wandering up and down, taking me in. "Of course I do. You look . . . *wow*, you look great."

"You too, Bradley."

He blinked. "What are you doing here?"

"I'm not sure. Just—"

Bradley's shock passed. "You shouldn't have come."

"Why?"

"Because. After what happened—"

He turned to walk away, and I noticed his limp, no doubt a result of the accident ten years ago.

"Bradley, please. Don't go."

He stopped but didn't turn. "Why?"

"I love you. If nothing else, that's why I'm here. *I love you.* I always have, always will. You're the love of my life. That's never changed."

"What about him?"

"Steve? He's married. We were over the moment I met you. Do you remember everything I told you? About us and how we were destined to be together?"

"I remember you and him kissing."

"It was a goodbye kiss. There was never anything else after that. I love you—how could there be?"

Bradley completed his turn, his wounded look clear, but he was listening. That mattered.

"All I'm asking for is a chance to prove to you that it's all true. We were great together. We could be again."

"What if I'm not single?" he asked.

"Then I'll leave. I don't want to cause you any more hurt."

"Too late; I'm hurt," he said. Seconds tolled silently with the weight of hours. "Okay, I'm single. You were a hard act to follow."

I stepped closer. "Then what do you say?"

He looked around before again meeting my hopeful gaze. Bradley shrugged. "It's great to see you again, Oliver."

I nodded and moved closer. He hugged me, and I fell into the protection of his arms.

It was a promising start for our new beginning.

About the Author

Raised on a healthy diet of creature double features and classic Science Fiction TV, Gregory L. Norris writes for national magazines, short story anthologies, novels, and the occasional episode for film and television. Norris writes *The Day After Tomorrow* series for Anderson Entertainment in the U.K. based on the Gerry Anderson NBC made-for-TV movie, which he watched and loved as a boy, and worked on Paramount's *Star Trek: Voyager* series as a screenwriter. Norris lives at the Outer Limits of New Hampshire's North Country in a century-old house called Xanadu with his giant rescue cat and emerald-eyed muse. For more information check out gregorynorris.com